Scam!

_____

By Stevie Turner

Title: Scam!

Copyright © 2023 Stevie Turner

ISBN: 978-1739401016

Cover by Carly McCracken

Dedication

Dedicated to all those who have been scammed out of their life savings. May you rise up again stronger than ever.

Table of Contents

Description

Lauren West and Ben Hughes are saving frantically for their forthcoming marriage and mortgage deposit. When Lauren sees an advert online from a firm of brokers extolling the profits to be gained by buying and selling Bitcoins, she is interested enough to pursue it further.

Lauren clicks on the advert. She is soon contacted by Paul Cash, a knowledgeable stockbroker whom Lauren trusts straight away. He is affable, plausible, and seemingly genuinely interested in her welfare. Lauren looks forward to making enough money to be able to surprise Ben and bring the date of their wedding forward, and also to put a deposit down on their ideal house.

What could possibly go wrong?

Chapter One - 2015

The next word I say will decide my future forever.

"Yes."

Surroundings in my shabby student digs fly away, and I no longer lie amongst rumpled and unwashed bed sheets in the front downstairs bedroom at 205a Cherry Hinton Road, Cambridge. Instead, for one brief moment, Ben's proposal lifts us both up over the snowy rooftops and lands us down on a deserted Caribbean island instead.

"Thank God for that! I was bricking it in case you said no!"

I laugh, cuddle closer to his chest and feel his warmth in the chill of the January evening, all the while twisting a long strand of white-blond hair at the back of his head around my forefinger.

"Why wouldn't I want to marry you? I need to snap you up before Diana bloody *Notlob* does." I pull a face. "Her legs are so bandy she couldn't stop a pig in a passage."

Ben sighs.

"Another saucer of milk, darling? Hey, let's not go through all that again. I've already told you... nothing ever happened between me and Diana Bolton."

"Forget it." I reach up and kiss the side of his neck. "You know I love you to the moon and back. Yes, yes ... yes!"

Two arms boasting enviable musculature squeeze me tightly.

"Awesome." Ben kisses the top of my head. "We'll have to save for a few years though, obviously. When we get our teaching posts then we'll be able to put a bit more money away. I know Mum and Dad will want me to work for what I want though. I was brought up that way."

"Me too." I reply, and lift myself up on one elbow. "I can't ask the parentals for more money anyway, because they've still got to put my sister through Uni yet."

Ben nods.

"My parents have it, but they just don't want to part with it. They had it tough at first, and Dad has always said it's the best way to learn value for money. Mum always tells me there's nothing more satisfying than buying a house that you've paid for yourself."

"Yeah, she's probably right." I sigh. "I just wish it would all happen *now*."

The usual throng of tourists jostle for position along King's Parade as we walk in crocodile form behind the Vice-Chancellor up to the Senate House wearing our hooded graduation robes in the bright June sunshine. I grin at Ben as he briefly looks over his shoulder and seeks me out right near the back with the foreign students as usual, as our surnames all end in either x, y or z.

Inside I search for Mum, Dad and my sister Linda, sitting proudly with cameras they aren't allowed to use. My little group of Ws wait seemingly forever for our turn, then walk four abreast up the aisle towards the Praelector, who speaks to the Vice Chancellor in Latin, but basically presents us individually to him. We kneel before the Vice Chancellor, who speaks in sonorous tones to the congregation.

"Te etiam admitto ad eundum gradum."

I know Mum and Dad will have no idea what is going on. We rise and bow to the Vice Chancellor and then exit through the Doctor's Door. I am handed my English/PGCE degree certificate and sigh with happiness as I search for Ben. We are both twenty three, engaged to be married, and now have Qualified Teacher Status after four long years of

9

study. The world is our lobster, or even oyster if we're lucky.

Ben, now a graduate Mathematics teacher, strides over to me as soon as we are freed from ceremony into the front garden of the Senate House. He has time to lift me up and swing me around before our parents and Linda file out as quickly as they can and descend, gloating, upon Ben and I to photograph us from every conceivable angle.

"Well done Lauren and Ben! I had no idea what they were all saying in there!"

Mum, bless her, has taken time and effort to straighten her dark curls which I have unfortunately inherited. The finished effect makes her look rather peculiar, and not like Mum at all.

"What have you done to your hair?" I laugh and hand her my certificate, already in its frame at extra cost. "I've never seen it like that."

"I had to straighten it or my hat would just perch on the top or fall off!" Mum chuckles while positioning Ben and I for another photograph.

Dad, the ever-gruff Yorkshireman looks proud but slightly self-conscious as he stands in the background with Linda, still at the blushing schoolgirl stage, and lets Mum enjoy her centre stage moment. Ben's mother comes over and gives me a quick kiss.

"I'm proud of the pair of you, but I'm sure Ben will need to get that ponytail cut off before he starts going to interviews."

"Well, that's up to him of course." I give my future mother-in-law a hug. "I rather like his long hair actually."

"Mum, it's not coming off." Ben shakes his head. "I'm going to be one of those trendy teachers who sits in the pub with his students."

"Ye Gods." Muriel Hughes *tuts* in mock annoyance and looks knowingly at her husband Geoff, "It's changed a bit since I first started work."

I snake an arm around Ben's waist underneath his robe.

"Well, I'll just be teaching little ones. Ben, you'll have to line the drinks up for me around four o'clock every day."

I like to tease Muriel, who I hope has a soft spot for me under her faintly brusque exterior. She rolls her eyes.

"My son and daughter-in-law-to-be are lushes."

Linda steps forward, while her enviably straight auburn locks fall to hide her face.

"Can I take a picture of you, Lauren?"

I disengage myself from Ben.

"Sure."

My sister takes after Dad; quiet and unassuming. I've inherited Mum's extrovert personality, which gets me into trouble sometimes as I can also be rather impulsive too, into the bargain. However, Linda's only 17 and still finding out about the world. We've never really argued, as Lin will always walk away from any confrontation, which tends to render it non-viable in a very short space of time.

I spend a few moments with my sister before it's time for group photographs with hoods down, more group photographs with hoods up, and then tea. I'm baking under my robe and can't wait to take it off. At one point I catch *Notlob* gazing at Ben with her doe-brown eyes. I'm still not sure if anything went on with those two apart from calculus, algebra, differential equations and geometry.

***

It's hard for us to say goodbye to our flat mates and move out from our digs. I feel a twinge of jealousy when I think of the new batch of carefree second year students moving into our bedroom from Halls in September. The time I've been dreading for months has come where Ben and I have to face the world and move in with his parents. Work and more work beckons until we can save enough money for a deposit. As much as I love Cambridge, house or even flat prices are beyond our means, therefore living in the city we love is unfortunately not an option.

Eltham seems drab after the bright lights of Cambridge, and I have the distinct feeling that Muriel and Geoff do not quite approve of their one and only son living in sin under their quite substantial roof. Mum and Dad are still in Yorkshire in the same little village they've lived in for 30 years, but at least in Eltham we're not too far from the centre of London by train. All our belongings are crammed into Ben's back bedroom. We frantically apply for teaching posts and take up summer jobs in the meantime; me working the tills in the local supermarket, and Ben playing lifeguard at the swimming pool. At night we try to have noiseless vanilla sex with one eye on the bedroom door that unfortunately never locks properly. The whole situation sucks.

Chapter Two

Ben has interest from Corelli College, which I find out was previously known as Kidbrooke Comprehensive. It's a large school taking in about 2000 students, and we discover it was the first comprehensive ever built. Apparently Jamie Oliver tried to tear pupils away from burgers and chips there in times gone by. Ben's as pleased as punch, and spends his lifeguard wages on a smart interview suit.

I secure an interview at Wyefield Primary School, a recently improved and upgraded edifice re-built from the ashes of a drab concrete council estate it previously stood on. All around are 'des res' apartments instead of the once vandalised blocks of flats and maisonettes. It's break time when I walk nervously through the playground full of hyper, noisy children, too busy screeching to even notice me.

I'm directed towards an obviously new and as yet unused classroom, currently serving as an inquisition chamber for several doubtless terrified and very junior would-be teachers. One of them exits as I go in. I give her a weak smile before coming face to face with the force that is Deborah Anderson, Head Teacher.

"Hi. I'm Lauren West." I try not to let my voice show my nervousness as I hold out my right hand. "Pleased to meet you."

The handshake is vigorous, and I get the impression of a firm but fair, no-nonsense kind of woman. Her hair is stone grey, but is cut into an attractive short style that flatters her fifty something oval shaped face.

"*Deborah.* Staff are all on first name terms here. Come and sit down, and we can have a chat."

I'm relieved and anxious to rest my shaky legs, and flop down rather too readily into the proffered chair. Deborah's eagle eyes take in my tailored suit, recent reddish low-lights, and hideously expensive Jimmy Choo slingbacks.

"I see from your CV that you're well qualified for this post."

"Yes." I nod. "First Class English degree and then a PGCE qualification, which of course included four months' teaching experience at Hillhunton School."

"Here at Wyefield we're interviewing for a Reception class teacher, as Yvonne Tobin has decided not to return after maternity leave. As you know, a newly qualified teacher will also need to undertake an induction year,

15

where I would evaluate their work and submit a report of the successful candidate's progress at the end of three terms to the local authority."

I quickly deduce that Yvonne Tobin's loss might possibly be my gain.

"I can assure you I have no intention of taking maternity leave for many years yet."

"Really?" A hint of a smile turned the corners of Deborah's mouth in an upwards direction. "So … where do you see yourself in ten years' time then?"

I decide to stick my neck out and make an impression.

"In *your* job."

Deborah laughs out loud.

"Jack Eastlake at Hillhunton sends a very favourable report of your work there." She leafs through her notes before looking up at me. "He thought you had quite a knack with the Reception class."

I relax a bit, cross my legs, and lean back in the chair.

She likes me…

"I love working with little ones."

"How about the parents though?" Deborah waggles one finger in my direction. "How would you cope with an angry six foot father looming over you, who doesn't like the fact that you've given his precious son low marks?"

"Well...I'd keep as calm as possible and try and reason with him. Does the school have panic buttons in the classrooms like Hillhunton did?"

Deborah nods.

"Of course." Deborah nods, "but luckily we haven't had to use them yet. One press of the button in the office or to the right of every class blackboard locks all the doors and windows, and all the windows are shatter-proof. It would need an axe to break any glass in this building. We also have a code phrase ...*Angela Draper's homework,* which when a member of staff hears this they would immediately phone the police. The school has improved no end since the sink estate around it was demolished. There aren't so many angry parents these days, but we decided it would be a good idea to keep all the security extras anyway."

"Wow." I reply. "I'd certainly use the button if I had to, but as you say, hopefully I won't need to press it."

***

I'm sweating with the effort of having answered all of Deborah's searching questions as I wait for the bus back to Eltham. On a whim I get off early at the start of the High Street and pop into Eltham Baths. Mel is at the reception desk.

"I just want to speak to Ben, if that's okay?"

Mel smiles and lets me pass through the entry barrier. When Ben sees me with my nose pressed up against the poolside's long glass windows, he signals to a colleague to take over before striding over to the emergency exit and popping his head round the door.

"What's up?"

I want to kiss him in my excitement.

"I've just had a fantastic interview at Wyefield …the head teacher and I got on really well!"

"That's great!" Ben nods. "Mum sent a text to say there's still no word from Corelli College, and I spent all that money on a bloody suit. Perhaps it *is* the ponytail." He gives it a tug. "Do you think I ought to cut it off?"

"No." I answer with a chuckle. "It wouldn't be *you* otherwise."

He looks over his shoulder.

"Anyway, I've got to go. My shift ends at five thirty." He gives me a quick peck on the cheek. "Speak to you later."

The High Street is teeming with afternoon shoppers, and I enjoy the slow stroll along its length before I turn left at Blunts Road and walk to the end. After crossing over Gourock Road and turning left into Glenhouse, I see my future in-laws' double fronted Edwardian house come into view at the end of the road on my right. I haven't yet been given a key, and so I ring the bell and wait for Muriel to twitch the net curtains at one of the front bay windows. She takes her time to answer the door.

"Lauren! Did the interview go well?"

The hallway carpet has been vacuumed again. I quickly whip off my heels before they leave holes in the shag pile.

"Yes, thanks." I nod. "Let's say I'm quietly hopeful."

"Fantastic!"

Muriel's joy is genuine, probably aided by the relief of knowing that Ben and I might soon be earning enough money to buy a place of our own.

"Can I help you with anything?"

I desperately want to get out of my interview clothes and into my usual garb of jeans and tee-shirt, but feel I need to be constantly thankful that Ben's parents have taken me in.

"Geoff's still working in the study. Dinner's on the go." Muriel shakes her head. "I expect you'd like to change and get over the stress of your day."

She's not far wrong.

"Cheers." I reply in pseudo-cheery tone. "I'll get some jeans on. Just give me a shout if you need any jobs done."

In the privacy of our bedroom I flop onto the duvet and wish for the thousandth time that Ben and I had our own place so that I do not have to be constantly on my best behaviour. Ben can see no wrong in living cheaply in the childhood home that he loves. We only need to pay towards the electric and gas bills, and Muriel cooks us dinner every night. But it's *her* choice of food cooked at a time of *her* choosing. Many would say we've got it made, but I beg to differ.

Chapter Three

The two week waiting on tenterhooks is worth it in the end. Both Ben and I secure teaching posts; Ben at Corelli College and me with the little ones at Wyefield Primary. There's a few more weeks of summer to enjoy before we begin our teaching careers, but ever mindful of the need to escape from Muriel and Geoff, we carry on with our temporary jobs. I open a savings account at the Nationwide Building Society to run alongside our joint current account, and before long we amass the pathetic sum of four hundred pounds.

"Only another thirty grand to go."

Ben laughs at my remark, and as we lie quietly in bed in each other's arms I broach a question which has been on my mind for some time.

"If we actually ask them for a loan, d'you think your parents would help us out with a few thousand perhaps? We could pay them back."

There is no immediate affirmative comment, and so before he even replies I know what the answer will be.

"No. It won't work. As I said before, Mum and Dad are all for being self-sufficient and learning the value of money. They'll probably pay a bit towards the wedding, but as for a mortgage deposit, forget it. Still no for your folks too?"

I try not to let my mood sink too low at the thought of being stuck with my in-laws for the foreseeable future. I give him a squeeze.

"They don't have that much money to splash around, and are already looking through Uni brochures with Linda. Looks like the banks of Mum and Dad are closed to us."

Ben chuckles.

"We'll get there. You'll just have to be patient. In the meantime you're stuck here with me."

I roll over on top of him and force a smile.

"Am I complaining?"

I kiss him, and he pins our bodies together with his arms. As he moves with an increasing rhythm inside me, I'm rather glad that Geoff's hearing isn't all it used to be and that Muriel has turned the TV up loud.

***

When my shift at the supermarket finishes, I always have to walk back along Eltham High Street past '*Brides to Be*' with its changing selection of sumptuous wedding gowns to die for in the shop window. I often loiter outside the shop for ages, just trying to imagine myself standing at the altar wearing one of them. The price tags are never displayed, as of course that would be unseemly and spoil the wonder of it all.

At the start of September I can bear the suspense no longer, and tentatively open the door to the shop. There's a wonderful smell of brand new tulle, organza and chiffon. I notice the assistant hovering hopefully next to a tearful mother near the back of the shop, who gazes lovingly at her daughter clad in a puffed and flouncy white creation, which to me resembles a meringue. The sales assistant clocks me with a quick glance and leaves the happy couple alone for a moment.

"Good afternoon." The assistant wears her best smile. "Can I help you?"

The mother sniffs and turns to look at me, and I want to run out again.

"Er… I'm just enquiring how much your wedding dresses are please."

""All different prices, but they range from about seven hundred and fifty pounds to somewhere around two thousand five hundred." She beams and gestures towards rails full of chiffon, crepe, silk and taffeta creations. "Take your time and look at these while I serve my customer."

She turns back to the mother and her meringue, and I pull up a few of the protective covers on the gowns, but they're all out of my price range. Despondent, I finger the fine lace and taffeta on a long sparkling dress and heave a sigh.

"Try it on if you like?"

The sales assistant has returned while Ben has been gazing adoringly at me at a virtual altar. I pull myself together.

"Can I?"

"Sure." The assistant nods. "Changing cubicles are at the back of the shop. I'm Brenda, by the way."

"Lauren." I reply with a smile.

The meringue has changed into a young twenty-something woman in jeans, trainers, and a jumper. She grins at me, then runs to hug her mother.

Trembling with excitement, I swap my supermarket uniform for a knockout £1850 wedding dress. It fits me in all the right places, and I have to admit that I look absolutely terrific. I sashay out into the changing area corridor, twirl about a bit, and watch my reflection in the mirror.

"You know, *Deirdre* is *so* you!"

The saleswoman claps her hands to emphasise her statement. For a brief moment I wonder who the hell Deirdre is, but then I realise it's the name of the dress. I quash the urge to giggle.

"Thanks. Are there any payment options?"

Brenda looks thoughtful.

"Sure. There's cash, bank card or credit card, but we don't take cheques anymore."

"No." I shake my head. "I mean monthly payments."

"Oh." Brenda's face falls and my heart sinks. "We don't do finance agreements or give credit, I'm afraid. You'd have to get a bank loan for that."

It's out of the question while we're trying to save. I reluctantly remove Deirdre from my person, return it to Brenda, and morph back into a supermarket worker.

Chapter Four - 2018

Resplendent in Deirdre's slightly cheaper younger
sister, I check my make-up for the last time in the bathroom
mirror before rustling out onto the upstairs landing of my
parents' house. Dad beams a smile wide enough to drive a
bus through.

"You look absolutely beautiful!"

"Thanks Dad." I brush an imaginary piece of fluff off
the shoulder of his three piece suit. "Thanks for
everything."

Bless him, he's nearly bankrupted himself to pay for
our wedding. At the last moment neither Mum nor Dad
would allow anybody else to chip in with the cost of it all.
This has helped our bank account no end, as we're now
only about fifteen thousand pounds off the thirty thousand
needed to secure our first home. We've been working hard
over the past few years, and now when the autumn term
begins my new Reception class will need to get used to

calling me *Mrs Hughes* instead of Miss West. It sounds strange even to me.

Meanwhile I'll have three weeks to get used to my new moniker before school starts. I tread carefully down the stairs towards where the chauffeur-driven Rolls Royce is waiting. Mum, Linda and the other bridesmaids have already gone ahead to the church. Ben and I have our faces on the place settings for the wedding breakfast, and so there's definitely no turning back now.

***

And here I am, as I have often pictured myself. I stand in sartorial splendor at the flower-bedecked altar with Ben's adoring gaze making me blush in front of the congregation. By the sounds of sniffing and snorting coming from behind me, there's not a dry eye in the place. The minister smiles at us, and I cannot wait to sit down; my legs have turned to jelly.

"In the presence of God, and before this congregation, Lauren and Ben have given their consent and made their marriage vows to each other. They have declared their marriage by the joining of hands and by the giving and receiving of rings. I therefore proclaim that they are husband and wife."

We've finally done it! Ben plants a big smackeroo on my lips, and I heave a sigh of relief. The minister mumbles his congratulations too, and some of the congregation clap noisily. I relax a bit when Linda's choir pipe up with a few songs as the new Mr and Mrs Hughes wobble off to the vestry with the nearest and dearest to sign the register.

I shoot my mother-in-law a grimace as she signs her name. We're still saving frantically, and unfortunately will still have to return to Muriel and Geoff's house following our honeymoon in Devon. After three years, Muriel and I rub each other up the wrong way, because there's one too many women in the house. I want to reach up and grab the stupid fascinator off her head and stamp on it. It's got to the point where I'd do anything to get the last few thousand and move into our own place and be free to do as we please, to make as much noise as we wish, and to eat dinner at a time of our own choosing. Ben says we're lucky to have had the chance of living cheaply for three years. I suppose he's right, but as far as I'm concerned I'd rather pay out even for a poky bedsit.

We walk arm-in-arm back up the aisle to another round of applause. Behind us Muriel and my father link arms and follow behind Geoff and Mum. I know Mum finds Muriel rather intimidating, but she seems to get on okay with

28

Geoff. Dad is his usual taciturn self. Goodness knows what Muriel thinks of *him*.

Ben and I grin inanely for the photographer before being showered in a ton of confetti, some of which finds its way down my cleavage. Ben grins.

"I'll pick it out later."

I've made sure that our first night as a married couple is not going to be spent under Muriel and Geoff's roof. As was our wish, our eighty wedding guests have all agreed to pay a little bit towards one night at the Oriental Mandarin Hotel in Knightsbridge for us instead of buying presents, and I know my in-laws generously made up the difference so I cannot complain too much. The room is hideously expensive (I've looked it up on Google), and so we're determined to enjoy the privacy and make the most of it before driving off for a week's stay in sunny Hayes, Cornwall.

We leave our guests dancing at the evening disco after we cut the cake. In the fluorescent glare of the hall's toilets I twirl my new gold band around my finger before changing into a more suitable travelling outfit than a wedding dress. We run out to the car park shrieking like banshees and holding each other's hands. I expect it's Linda and the other bridesmaids who have tied a jumble of old tins to the back bumper of our Skoda. My sister holds up her long dress as she runs to catch up with us, panting slightly.

"See you soon, Lauren!"

I let go of Ben's hand and give her a hug.

"Cheers for the cans, but I won't be able to stand them rattling all the way to Knightsbridge. We'll have to cut them off."

"Shame!" She laughs. "After all the trouble I went to!"

The Skoda bursts into life and Ben backs out onto the road. I can see Mum and Dad waving goodbye on the steps of the community hall. I suddenly feel like crying, but I don't know why.

***

The six foot bed is dressed and draped in sumptuous splendour. It's a room to die for. I look around the opulent surroundings in wonder as Ben lifts me up and carries me over the threshold of room 492 at the Oriental Mandarin hotel.

"I read once that Jon Bon Jovi sometimes stays here when he has a UK concert."

With some relief Ben lowers his burden onto the satin coverlet.

"Do you think he's slept in this bed then?"

I shrug and hold my arms out to him, and he flops on top of me.

"Who cares? I always preferred Richie anyway."

We kiss passionately and soon forget who may or may not have stayed in our room, because for the next 24 hours it belongs to just me and Ben.

***

The Skoda just about makes the long drive to our hotel at Hayes the next day without overheating in nose to tail traffic on the A30. Ben's parents have paid for a room for us in a rather nice five star hotel near the beach. However, there's a change in the weather on the second day. We listen to the patter of raindrops against the window, and slip the 'Do not disturb' sign over the doorknob. It's rather wonderful to stay in bed all morning and get to know each other even better.

Chapter Five

I'm ready for the 'lack of suntan' jokes from friends on our return to Eltham, but by and large everybody tactfully steers clear of asking us what we've been doing on our honeymoon.

It's a little over a week until the start of a new school term. I pop into the Nationwide to check how much interest has been paid on our savings. It's not much, and we're still fifteen thousand pounds short of putting a deposit on a property around the three hundred thousand mark.

Back at Muriel and Geoff's I fire up the computer in our bedroom to check out local evening vacancies that do not include shift work. The home page goes straight to MSN, and I give a *tut* of annoyance because Ben must have changed it again. An article catches my eye featuring a well-known actress, who extols the virtues of Bitcoins. I read on how she has made the quickest five thousand pounds ever, through buying and selling Bitcoins on the stock market. Below the actress' grinning features in large print is a banner advertising brokers FinMoyle with the tempting words 'Find Out More'.

Intrigued, I figure if a famous actress has endorsed a company, then it must be genuine. There's an accompanying video, where more smiling celebrities rave about digital currency and how Brexit has devalued the pound so badly that the only way to make a profit is to invest in Bitcoins.

I am hooked. Our new flat materializes before my eyes. I click on the 'Find Out More' button and add my email address. Within a short time an email notification pops up at the bottom of my screen. I have an email from a John Lenz at FinMoyle asking for my phone number. Virtually as soon as I type in my mobile phone details it starts to ring with an unidentified London number.

"Hi. Is that Lauren? This is Paul Cash from FinMoyle."

The voice is deep and raspy and I'm unable to identify his accent.

"Yes." I reply. "You have the right surname then."

There is a throaty laugh at the other end of the line.

"Yeah, I have to agree with you. So… tell me a little bit about yourself and why you're interested in FinMoyle. Where did you find us, by the way?"

He seems friendly, and I open up a bit.

"I saw the advert on MSN, where Kath Willet talks about the profit she's made by buying Bitcoins."

"Ah yes." Paul replies. "A nice little nest egg for her. So you want to do the same?"

There's a noise in the background that I cannot identify. I can only describe it as the sound of a stuck stylus in the groove of on an old vinyl record, the like of which my grandmother used to play.

"Yes." I agree, as pound signs flash before my eyes. "My husband and I want to move out of his parents' house and buy our own place. We've been saving up for a mortgage deposit, but it's not enough yet."

"Ah. I see." Paul clears his throat before continuing. "It's a bit noisy here in the trading room. I'm going to walk to my office, so bear with me."

There is a pause, and the background din disappears.

"That's better. So Lauren… you live with your in-laws?"

"That's right." I sigh. "I can't wait to move out."

He chuckles.

"But it's given you time to save up… no?"

"Well, yeah, I suppose so." I reply. "But we need another fifteen thousand at least."

"Well, you can't go wrong by investing in Bitcoins." Paul answers. "But I have to warn all my clients that stock market prices can go down as well as up, but on the whole Bitcoins are a good investment."

"Then I'd like to buy some."

My voice is breathy with excitement. Ben will be home from his casual job at Eltham Baths soon. I don't want him to know anything until I present him with at least a ten thousand pound windfall. Paul interrupts my thoughts, and I want to find out more about him.

"I cannot place your accent." I venture.

"I'm American, can't you tell?" Paul replies easily. "I was born in Chicago, but am now based in London. Just to inform you, if you would like me to manage your account I do take six percent of your profits. However, you can run your trading account yourself if you have the knowledge?"

Shares, hedge funds and stock markets are way beyond me. I quickly respond to his question.

"Oh no, I have no idea about stocks and shares. I'm a primary school teacher. I would have to let you manage my account."

"A teacher?" Paul sounds impressed. "Little ones or big ones?"

"Ha, just primary school children." I chuckle. "Wyefield Primary is a great school not too far from where I live. So you'll be able to manage my account then?"

"That'll be fine." Paul's voice is authoritative and somehow soothing. "My assistant will be in touch quite soon with a link to your new trading account. We will take it from there. When is a good time to speak to you? During the day? Evenings?"

My mind races. Ben is usually home later than me on a school day, as he likes to prepare the next day's lesson before he leaves. I tend to make my plans at the end of the day.

"Between four and five o'clock on weekday afternoons." I reply. "School begins on Monday, so please don't phone until then. I want to present my husband with a fat cheque as a surprise."

There's another throaty laugh.

"Okay. On Monday afternoon I'll phone you, and go through your trading account. There's a lot to take in at first, but it'll become clearer after a few months."

I sigh.

"I hope so. Thanks for your call. Speak to you on Monday."

When the call ends I sit back in the chair and slowly exhale. I'm tingling with the excitement of finally being able to go flat-hunting. Houses are still out of our price range of course, so it'll be a case of upsizing in a few years' time when our flat has made enough profit. I hug myself and grin; Ben is going to be so pleased with his new wife's shrewd investments!

Chapter Six

On the dot of four o'clock the following Monday afternoon, my mobile phone rings. I'm tired after the first day back at school, and am lazing on our bed when I see Paul's number flashing on my display screen. Ben is still at Corelli College, Muriel is gardening, and Geoff is out doing whatever Geoff does. I pick up the phone.

"Hi Paul."

"Hey Lauren!" Paul's voice is upbeat. "Did you have a good weekend?"

There's that stuck stylus noise in the background again. I suddenly remember how my grandmother used to put a ten pence piece on top of it before she came around to accepting CD players.

"Great thanks. Did you?"

"You're the first customer that's ever bothered to ask me that." Paul replies with a chuckle. "The answer is yes, fine thank you, and if you check your email account you'll see that my assistant Lance Jackson has sent you a link so that you can open your trading account."

"Okay. Just let me switch on the computer."

I feel a pang of excitement shoot through my veins as I log in and open up my emails. Sure enough the latest message is from Lance@FinMoyle, who has sent a link to my new trading account, a user number, and a Managed Account Agreement. I quickly scan the agreement while my heart thumps with excitement:

(Name of Account Holder) _Lauren Hughes

Below are the Terms and Conditions as well as Profit/Risk scale that we offer as part of a Managed trading account:

1. Trading period under the managed account will last a minimum of four calendar months.

2. The client can withdraw up to ten percent from the account value as long as there are no open trades. (This is valid during the first four months and does not include profit withdraws)

3. Profit fee of six percent of the Profit made Monthly.

4. Trading will be done only by the Assigned Account Manager.

5. Profit withdraws will be issued once in every calendar month, on a date predetermined by the Client and the Account Manager.

6. Every trade is part of a group and cannot be closed before due time.

7. In order to claim profit, the client must have all required documents approved and account fully verified.

8. The leverage of trading will be up to 1:400 (please specify between 1:25 - 1:400) on the clients deposited amount.

9. The maximum risk in trading can be up to the actual deposited amount. The account will be protected by the company from negative balance.

Disclaimer: HIGH RISK WARNING: Trading Foreign Exchange (Forex) and Contracts For Differences (CFD's) is highly speculative, carries a high level of risk and may not be suitable for all investors. You may sustain a loss of some or all of your invested capital, therefore, you should not speculate with capital that you cannot afford to lose. You should be aware of all the risks associated with trading on margin.

The client gives approval and consent to his account manager to open 25 (please specify an amount of trades between 10-25) positions on his behalf on a daily basis. According to different opportunities in the market.

11. The client gives authorization and consent to his account manager to open positions on his behalf, with volume trade of 10 (please specify volume range between 0.25 - 100.00 LOT).

12. The client authorizes his account manager to open
positions for the following CFD's assets on his behalf:
(Please specify Y/N)
FOREX _y____ Crypto__y___ Commodities___y__
Stocks___y__ Indices__y___
Please confirm that you have understood and agree to
these conditions and understand the trading risks involved
by replying to the Email that this file has been attached to.
This agreement is subject to the terms and conditions as it
appears on the website FinMoyle.com

I don't understand some of the technical jargon, but I am reassured when reading that my account will be protected from a negative balance.

"Everything okay?"

Paul's voice shoots me back to the present.

"Oh, yes. I was just reading the agreement."

"Sure. If you could sign that at the bottom and send it back to me at your leisure, then that'll be great. For now, just click on the link and open up your new trading account."

"Okay. Will do."

The click leads me to a totally unfamiliar dashboard that I assume would only be recognised by a stock broker. To me it might just as well be written in Chinese.

"I don't understand it at all."

Paul laughs.

"That's why you've asked me to manage it for you? No?"

"Yes, of course." I reply. "But I'd like to know how you buy and sell on the stock market though."

"I can show you, but I'd need to take over your screen. It's easy to do via *Any Desk*. Would you like to go ahead? You might even be able to do it yourself after a few months."

His voice is pleasant, but I still cannot place the accent. Stocks and shares and numbers blink in front of my eyes. I was only ever any good with words.

"Yes, okay, do go ahead."

Paul continues as I stare at the screen.

"Search for *Any Desk*, click on '*free download for personal use*' and then download it. You'll then be given an *Any Desk* number. Let me know what it is."

It's easy enough to log into the site. Sure enough a number pops up after I have downloaded the *Any Desk* programme.

"It's nine three six, one seven two."

Before my eyes the cursor moves on its own. It minimises *Any Desk* and my desktop comes into view.

"You've got a busy desktop screen."

I feel a slight twinge of annoyance that Paul is nosing about on my computer.

"Shouldn't you be looking at my trading account instead?"

I am relieved when straight away he moves the cursor to click back onto the FinMoyle screen.

"Would you like me to talk you through it all?"

I can hear Muriel coming upstairs. The inner walls are not terribly thick.

"No. Leave it now. I'll read the agreement properly and then send it back to you."

"Great." Paul's voice sounds positive in my ear. "As soon as I receive it, then we can move forward and begin trading. Read it over tonight, and I'll phone you tomorrow at the same time."

There's a knock on my bedroom door. I end the call and turn off the computer's monitor.

"Hi Muriel!"

My mother-in-law pops her head around the door.

"There's chicken curry for dinner tonight at six o'clock."

I'm not too keen on curry, and she knows it.

"I'll grab a sandwich, thanks."

I cannot wait to make a killing on the stock market and move out.

Chapter Seven

True to his word, Paul's number flashes up on my phone at four o'clock the next day.

"Hi Paul." I hold my phone in one hand and log in to the computer with the other. "Did you receive the agreement I sent?"

"Yes, I did. We're all good to go."

"Great." I reply. "What do you want me to do?"

"Go into *Any Desk* again. This time when you log into FinMoyle I'll show you how to add in all your personal details and then buy the *Smart Bits* you'll need to start trading on *Forex*. We'll start small and see how we go."

"Sounds okay." I am reassured. "Starting small is how I'd like to proceed."

I log into FinMoyle and then Paul takes over.

"Just add your name, address, and date of birth to your account for starters. There's also the section where you can scan in a picture of both sides of your bank card, but again, you can do that at your leisure. Don't worry, you can blank out the long number if you wish. I'll also need you to scan in your passport and a utility bill to prove your identity and your address. It's standard practice."

Inputting my details is easy enough, although I'm aware that he must be viewing everything I type.

"Thanks for that. I'll wait to receive the other scanned documents." He moves the cursor. "As you can see, I'm now going into the *Buy Smart Bits* screen. This is where you'll need to add details of your bank card."

I'm a little perturbed as I type in my numbers, which do not appear to be encrypted. Paul speaks as soon as I'm finished.

"Great. What about starting with two hundred and fifty pounds? The commission on that will only buy me a pack of cigarettes though."

It's not too much money for me to lose if it all goes Pete Tong. I'm not greedy and I don't really care about Paul's commission. I'd rather make sure that trading on *Forex* is a guaranteed way to earn a little bit of profit.

"Okay." I reply. "Let's do it."

Before too much time has gone by I am £250 down. Paul clears his throat.

"I'll start trading for you straight away. US Dollars. I won't take any risks, and in three days when I sell, your account will see a small profit. Not much, but it's a start.

46

I'll speak to you again in three days, and we'll log in to your account again and you'll be able to see how much profit you've made."

"Thanks."

I'm pleased at how Paul is taking things slowly. I end the call and close down the computer.

***

We're sitting at the dinner table the following evening when I can feel my mobile phone vibrating. I take it out of my pocket just as Ben's loaded fork pauses in its journey towards his mouth.

"Who's that?"

I glance down quickly at the phone in my lap. Paul's number flashes up on the screen.

"Oh, it's Deborah from the school. Sorry about this, I'll just take it upstairs. They're probably short staffed again."

I make a hurried exit and take the stairs two at a time to my computer, and switch it on.

"Hello?"

I try to make the greeting sound as offhand has possible.

"Lauren! Am I interrupting anything? Thanks for uploading your passport details. I still need a utility bill by the way."

His voice is as cheerful and upbeat as ever. I exhale loudly.

"Yes. We're eating dinner. You said you wouldn't phone for another three days. My husband and I help to pay some of the bills, but we don't own the house as we live with his parents. Therefore I can send a utility bill, but it will have their names on. Is that okay?"

"Okay, but listen. This is very exciting. I've had insider information, the kind that only comes once or twice a year. There's a chance to make a huge amount of money, and I didn't want you to miss out. As you know, the London Liverpool Bank has been failing recently. It's all in the news so you can look it up on Google, but we've had info this afternoon that they've agreed to a merger. The price of shares will rise considerably the day after tomorrow, and that info is absolutely guaranteed. For an investment of say, ten K, your profits would be around a hundred and fifty K."

I sit up straighter in the chair.

"A hundred and fifty thousand pounds profit?"

"Absolutely. Talk it over with your husband and give me a call back, but there's no time to lose."

Ten thousand pounds is nearly half of our savings. Ben would be appalled, but I can already imagine the look of surprise on his face as I hand him a £150,000 cheque.

"I'll think about it."

Paul sighs.

"Don't think too long. Email me your decision as soon as you can, and we'll take it from there. If the answer is yes, then you'll need to log into the FinMoyle website. I can take over your screen again and help you with the investment."

"If I decide, it'll be tomorrow not today. I'll let you know."

I end the conversation and run downstairs. Muriel has put a plate over my dinner, and they have almost finished eating. Ben puts down his knife and fork and smiles at me.

"Problems?"

"Nothing I can't handle." I take my place at the table again. "Sorry about that."

My mind is whirring in top gear as I mechanically eat the rest of my food. To make such a huge profit would mean that Ben and I could move out straight away and even rent while we're house-hunting.

"What do you think, Lauren?"

The sound of my name causes me to look up blankly at my mother-in-law, who has asked me a question I haven't even heard.

Chapter Eight

I cannot relax. Beside me Ben slumbers the sleep of the unconcerned. I've done my homework, and the London Liverpool Bank is indeed in dire financial straits. My brain fires on all cylinders as I imagine the type of house we could buy with such a large deposit. We could even hold some money back and have an all-inclusive holiday or cruise. The possibilities are endless.

The digital clock reads four thirty. In two hours I must get up, act normally and drive to school. I make a final decision whether or not to go ahead with the investment, and after that fall into a fitful sleep until the alarm sounds.

I'm too jittery to eat breakfast. Muriel enquires why I'm starting the day on just strong coffee, but Ben is used to my sometimes irritable stomach and goes off to work without suspecting a thing.

At school, the children are unusually restless, just like me, and I have trouble keeping them in their seats. When it's lunch time I eat on the go and drive back to Eltham High Street. There's a queue at the Nationwide Building Society, and my heart is pounding as I wait to ask the assistant to transfer ten thousand pounds to my current account. For a few hours my account will now boast £12,504.76, as pay day has just been and gone too. When the deed is done and she returns my savings book, I see that we now have only eight thousand quid left. I laughingly ask her what the interest rate would be on one hundred and fifty thousand pounds, but she just smiles and moves on to the next customer.

At four thirty Paul rings just as I return home. One part of me had hoped he wouldn't call, but the other half could not wait to get it over with.

"Hi Lauren!"

He's eager to do business, I can tell. I close our bedroom door and switch on the computer.

"Hello Paul, I'm just logging in."

"Great!" he replies with gusto. "I take it you've decided to invest?"

It's make or break time…

"Er… yes."

"Don't sound so doubtful!" Paul laughs. "It's a cinch, as they say in my hometown."

I've no idea what a cinch is. I'm suddenly nervous as hell and worried about whether or not I'm doing the right thing.

"Are you sure the share price is going up?"

"Absolutely." Paul replies. "As I told you before, I've had insider information, which is never wrong, and anyway, I'll be managing your account for you for the six percent commission we agreed upon. Go to *Any Desk* now, and tell me the number that you see in the box."

I am reassured. With trembling fingers I type in my password and then log in to *Any Desk*.

"One Seven Three Two Nine."

He takes over my screen in an instant.

"Sign into your trading account, and then go to the *Buy Smart Bits* page. You'll need your bank card to pop in all the details."

I forage about in my handbag for the Nationwide card. Downstairs I hear a key turning in the front door and Ben's voice as he shouts out a greeting, then Muriel's reply. Paul calls my attention back to the screen.

"Add your card's long number, the expiry date and the three numbers on the back."

Strangely enough, again the numbers are not encrypted. There is silence on the line, and I hold my breath as ten thousand Smart Bits are purchased.

"Well done, Lauren. In a couple of days you'll be a hundred and fifty thou richer, less my six percent of course."

"I can hardly bear the excitement!" I reply with a laugh. "I've got to go now, but I'll await your call."

"Sure thing. I'll call around four thirty on Friday."

I log off and Paul hangs up just as Ben bursts into the room.

"Hi, love." He flops onto the bed. "Had a good day?"

"Not bad." I smile at him. "How about you?"

Ben yawns.

"I had to cover a Year Ten Chemistry lesson today. Ian Marsh set light to a rubbish bin with a Bunsen burner."

"Things never change then." I laugh. "Liz Chalmers did something like that when I was at school, as I remember. We were all made to stay behind at three o'clock."

"Can't do that now, it's lunchtime detentions these days. Who was that on the phone? I heard you talking."

"Oh, just Deborah." I reply with a shrug. "School stuff."

"Of which I don't want to do any more of until later on." Ben jumps up and comes over to give me a cuddle.

"I've a stack of books to mark after dinner, but now I want to give my wife a kiss."

I wrap my arms around him; dear uncomplicated Ben. I love him dearly, and look forward to the day after tomorrow when I can show him what a clever girl I've been.

Chapter Nine

When school ends on Friday afternoon, the children are just as relieved as I am to escape their confines. I exchange a few pleasantries with Deborah and with a few mothers hanging around in the playground, then jump in the car and drive back as fast as legally possible to await Paul's telephone call.

By the time Ben arrives at 5:15pm with his arms full of books to mark, Paul has still not called. I want to surprise Ben, and so keep my mobile phone near to me, ready to run to somewhere private.

I begin to worry after dinner. It's now 6:45 pm and my phone lies silent in the pocket of my jeans as Ben and I wash up the dishes.

"You're quiet tonight." Ben, tea towel in hand, gives me a peck on the cheek. "What's up?"

"Oh, just tired. It's been a long week."

"Yeah, me too." Ben gives me a quick kiss. "We can have a nice lie in tomorrow."

When Ben is in the en-suite shower, I quickly turn on our computer and type *'FinMoyle'* into Google.

Immediately there are links to forums where people ask if the company is accredited and genuine. My heart begins to pound in alarm as I read answers from people who have lost money that FinMoyle is not regulated by the Financial Conduct Authority, and to only deal with companies who boast the FCA logo. I delve deeper and discover that FinMoyle's location is a P.O box in St. Vincent & the Grenadines, along with 150 other so-called 'financial' companies all using the same address.

I feel sick. Ben sings gaily in the shower as it slowly dawns on me that I've been incredibly stupid and through my own greed have lost us over half of our precious mortgage deposit. I quickly dial Paul's number, but the phone has a disconnected tone.

My fingers tremble as I type the two passwords which will enable me to log in to the Nationwide Bank. Through tears of anger at my own stupidity I see the remainder of our savings are still safe, but there has been an online purchase which I have not made and most of my recently deposited wages are missing.

I put a stop on my bank card, send a secure message to the effect that I have been a victim of a scam, and just for good measure make a note of the number to ring to report lost or stolen cards. I look at the FinMoyle website again while I inwardly seethe with anger, partly at myself, but also at the low life that calls himself Paul Cash, if indeed that is his real name.

Ben comes out of the shower as I sit, head in hands, at the computer. He comes over to me and puts an arm around my shoulders.

"Are you crying? What's the matter?"

I cannot bear to tell him, but tell him I must. The tears fall faster and my breath comes in sobs.

"I -I've been so stupid!"

"Why?"

My husband has no idea that I am about to wreck his weekend. I wipe my eyes and try unsuccessfully to regain my composure.

"He told me he had insider information... that I could make a hundred and fifty grand!"

"*Who* told you?" Ben's voice rises as he drops to his knees, grips my shoulders, and stares hard into my face. "What are you talking about?"

"Ben..." A fresh wave of tears erupt and fall down my cheeks. "I've been the victim of a scam. He took ten thousand pounds. I'm so sorry!"

"What?" Ben looks at me incredulously. "You're fucking joking, right?"

I shake my head.

"I only wish I was. His name, well the name he gave me anyway, is Paul Cash. The company is FinMoyle." I point to the computer. "It's there on the screen."

Ben sinks to the floor and looks up at me.

"How could you be so thick as to believe something like that? Why didn't you speak to *me* first?"

"I wanted to surprise you!" I sob. "I want to move out of here so badly! I thought he was the real deal. He came over as genuine. His phone's switched off now or disconnected."

"Yeah, I bet it is." Ben snakes a hand slowly through his wet hair and sighs. "Lauren, I really don't know what to say."

Suddenly another thought crashes through my brain.

"Oh God, I scanned over my passport details as well."

"You stupid woman!" Ben stands up and shakes his head in disbelief. "They've probably cloned it already. You'll need to go online and cancel it right now. What else did you give him?"

I'm distraught at his anger. I turn towards the computer and dissolve into floods of tears.

"This address! I gave him Muriel and Geoff's address!"

"Oh sweet Jesus." Ben shakes his head. "What a fucking mess!"

I hear footsteps outside on the landing.

"Everything alright?"

I imagine Muriel's ear up against the door.

"Yes!" I shout, before Ben has a chance to reply. "We're absolutely fine!"

Chapter Ten

I'm the first one in the queue when the Nationwide opens on Saturday morning. Ben isn't speaking to me, and I'm glad to get out of the house. I rush to the counter before anybody else has a chance to overtake me.

"I need to speak to somebody. I've been a victim of fraud."

I am directed towards a young woman who sits at a desk behind a privacy screen. She smiles at me.

"Hello? I'm Diane. Can I help you?"

"Yes please." I flop down in the chair opposite her. "I've lost ten thousand pounds and some of my wages through a scam. I'm hoping to be able to get the money back?"

The smile falters on her face.

"How did you pay the ten thousand?"

I detect a glimmer of hope.

"Online via my card."

"We'll certainly look into it for you, but I must be frank, if you paid willingly and entered the CVC number on the back of the card, then it's very unlikely the money will be returned. However, if your wages have been taken without your consent, then there's a chance they can be returned. I take it you have put a stop on your bank card?"

"Yes, I did that yesterday. I just checked on my phone, and the ten grand is still showing in my account!" My voice sounds desperate. "Can't you stop the purchase going through?"

The woman shakes her head.

"We have to wait until the money has gone from your account before we can do anything."

"That's ridiculous!" I'm shouting now, immune to the stares of customers in the queue. "Surely you can put a stop on it?"

"Not if you paid willingly, and entered your passwords and CVC number."

I want to cry again in frustration. I give her my account details and stand up.

"Please phone my mobile the minute you have an answer. I also want to close that bank account and transfer the money to a new account and start again."

***

I'm unwilling to return to the house where Muriel is watching and waiting for any other signs that Ben and I are not getting along, so I amble along the High Street, trying to calm down. I end up at the church on the crossroads where I find a seat amongst the Victorian graves. I close my eyes and let the warm autumn sun play on my face. I'm still sitting there an hour later when my mobile phone rings.

"Hello?"

"Mrs Hughes?"

"Yes."

"It's Diane from the Nationwide."

I feel a surge of hope.

"Have you been able to return the money to my account?"

There's a slight hesitation, and my heart sinks.

"I'm afraid we cannot do that. We've looked into this, and it seems to us as though you've made genuine purchases. Your CVC number was used, which gives it authentication. We'll set up a new account for you as you requested, but I'm sorry... we cannot refund the money. Try reporting this to Action For Fraud, who may be able to help."

I end the call and try not to cry again as I trudge back to Muriel and Geoff's house, where I find Ben sitting with his parents in the front room. There's an unpleasant atmosphere, and instinctively I know that Ben has just told them what I've done. All three barely acknowledge my presence as I walk past them towards the kitchen, where I sit at the table and let my tears fall freely into a welcome cup of hot coffee. Ben appears at the door, then comes to the table and sits opposite me.

"Mum and Dad are furious and want us out of here. I can't blame them really... you've given some toe rag their address."

"What you're saying is that Muriel wants *me* out of here." I sigh and look over at him. "I can't imagine she wants to kick *you* out, and Geoff probably hasn't even got a say in it. Anyway, how can we move out now? If we rent somewhere we'll never be able to save up for a deposit."

Ben shrugs.

"Well, that's *your* fault for being so impulsive, isn't it? Mum and Dad certainly won't help us financially now. We'll have to use some of our remaining money for a month's rent in advance and for furnishing a flat."

I wipe my eyes with a tissue.

"Fine. I can't wait to get out of here. Shall we go down to the estate agent's in the High Street today then and see what they've got? After that I'm going to go online and type out a report to Action For Fraud. The Nationwide told me to contact them."

"*I'll* sort a place out for us to rent." Ben replies. "Who knows what dodgy company *you'll* give our details to?"

I feel useless and stupid, and wish I could turn the clock back. The only glimmer of hope on the horizon is the fact that at last we can escape the clutches of Muriel and Geoff.

Chapter Eleven

Ben disappears after lunch, supposedly to find us somewhere else to live. He's inwardly fuming with anger. Neither Muriel nor Geoff have much to say to me, and so I settle down at the computer to contact Action For Fraud.

There's an in-depth form to fill out. There's no proper address for FinMoyle, apart from the P.O address at Kingston Beachtown, St. Vincent. However, I can add the FinMoyle website address and Paul Cash's London telephone numbers for the police to check out, and I will be able to add the Managed Account Agreement I was sent if I am asked to do so in the future. It seems any investigation the police will do might take at least twenty eight days.

It's a nice afternoon, and I have no intention of sitting in our bedroom for the rest of the day. I slink out of the front door, avoiding my in-laws who are weeding in the back garden, and head off with the hope of catching sight of Ben in one of the many estate agents premises dotted along the High Street.

His blond hair is easy to spot through a shop window, and he doesn't look around when I walk through the front door of Carter Jonas. The estate agent looks up enquiringly as I take a seat next to Ben.

"Don't worry, I'm not gate-crashing." I point towards Ben. "I'm his wife."

Ben gives me a thin smile and turns back to the young woman behind the desk.

"So... what have you got on your books for around nine hundred to a thousand pounds per month?"

This sounds a huge amount of money to me, and I'm not happy.

"Surely that's too much for a flat?" I enquire tentatively. "We need to pay less than that if we're going to save for a mortgage deposit."

Ben shoots me a withering look.

"I'm not going to live in some poky flat, and we'll never be able to save up for a deposit now, so we might as well just rent."

His offhand manner and cold stare chills me to the bone.

"Can we at least talk about this first?"

The estate agent looks as though she wants to be somewhere else. I feel her embarrassment as Ben shakes his head.

"What's the point? We'll view a few houses and then we can pick the best one."

Suddenly I'm downright angry at his controlling attitude. I stand up.

"We all make mistakes! Nobody's perfect! Just because I made one fucking mistake, don't punish me forever!"

All heads turn in my direction. Ben's surprise registers on his face for an instant before the impassive mask reappears. He gets to his feet, kills me dead with his eyes, and walks out of the shop. I make a vain attempt to regain my composure and sit back down, as the estate agent and several other staff and customers try to act as if nothing has happened. Trembling slightly, I look straight at the estate agent.

"Show me what you've got. I want to look at some properties this afternoon."

"Sure." She replies, with not even a vestige of a smirk. "You might like this one, it's just become available." She reaches over and pulls a piece of paper from the printer. "What do you think?"

I look at what appears to be a 1930s semi- detached house in good repair and with a neat front garden and off-street parking.

"Where is it?"

"Broad Walk, Kidbrooke." The estate agent checks details on her computer. "Near the school – Corelli College. Do you know it?"

I nod.

"Yes, my husband works there. At least he won't have to travel far to get to work, and from there I could walk to the school that I teach in too."

"Perfect!" The estate agent beams a smile big enough to light up the sky. "It's nine hundred and fifty pounds per month."

My impulsive nature comes to the fore again.

"I'll take it. I'll just nip to the Nationwide and transfer some money over to my current account."

"Don't you want to see it first?"

"Of course." I reply quickly. "But I don't want anybody else to get their hands on it. I'll put a refundable deposit down straight away, if I'm allowed to do that?"

"Yes, that's okay." The estate agent begins typing. "And we'll need a month's rent in advance if you decide to go ahead, but for now two hundred and fifty pounds will secure it for you."

***

There's a smell of fresh paint when I walk through the door. Straight away I love the leaded bay windows in the front of the house, the separate dining and utility rooms, and four large bedrooms upstairs giving us plenty of storage space until children start coming along.

"I love it."

The estate agent looks smug, as though she's mentally calculating her commission.

"I'll need both you and your husband's details and signatures, bank info, and work references please. Other than that, it's good to go. Have you got much furniture?"

"Not really." I shake my head. "But at least we'll have our own place to put it in when we do get some."

My angry mood has dissipated by the time I return to Muriel and Geoff's house. I've signed on the dotted line, and the deal is done. Ben can like it or lump it.

Chapter Twelve

Ben's not around when I get back and doesn't return until just before dinner, and so I make the big announcement just as Muriel serves up chicken casserole and rice.

"We'll be moving out soon. I've found a semi to rent near to Corelli College. Ben, you'll need to go back again to see the estate agent to sign a few forms and provide references."

There's a lukewarm reaction to my statement. Ben shrugs.

"I'm going to have to see it before I give the okay. You can't go making decisions for both of us without consulting me."

Muriel is listening intently, and I force the sweetest smile I can manage.

"Well… if you hadn't had a paddy and stormed out, you could have seen the house this afternoon when *I* did."

"Carter Jonas will be open tomorrow." Ben stuffs a lump of chicken in his mouth. "I'll be able to see it then."

We finish the meal in silence, and my offer to wash up afterwards is dismissed. I don't fancy sitting in the front room all evening looking at three long faces, and so I soak in the bath for a while before curling up on our bed with a book. Ben comes up just before midnight. I've been expecting his arrival for some time, and I'm wide awake with apprehension. He's in his dressing gown and smells of shampoo and shower gel. He throws off the gown and gets into bed, and I want to cuddle up to his bare chest like I always do. However, he turns on one side away from me. I sigh as I lie on my back and stare at the ceiling.

"You'll like the house. It's great."

There's no reply. Pretty soon his breathing is deep and even, but having been anxious for a few hours, I'm unable to sleep. I'm also peckish, and now that the house is still, the idea of a quiet cup of tea and a piece of toast moves more to the forefront of my thoughts.

I climb gingerly out of bed, then throw on a robe and pad downstairs. The fluorescent bulb in the kitchen splutters into life, throwing a harsh light on to Muriel's ultra-clean work surfaces. I feel like opening every packet and tin and throwing their contents any which way I can. Instead I boil the kettle and get some milk from the fridge.

"One sugar in mine, please."

Geoff appears in the doorway just as I mentally squirt a bottle of tomato sauce at the wallpaper. I smile at my father-in-law.

"I didn't hear you come down."

"I fell asleep in the front room. Muriel went up ages ago."

He's affable enough, and I breathe a sigh of relief.

"Sorry about the upset at dinner time. We'll get over it."

Geoff waves away my concern.

"I've transferred twenty thousand pounds to your bank account, so I don't want to hear another word about any of it."

I stand there open-mouthed in surprise for a moment.

"No, no, please! It's up to me to replace it, and I lost ten thousand, not twenty!"

"We all make mistakes when we're young." Geoff rolls his eyes briefly. "I married Muriel for starters, didn't I?"

I don't know whether to snort with laughter or remain serious. Instead I concentrate on pouring milk into two mugs of tea.

"You've both been very kind in letting me stay here, but it's not right for me to take all that money."

"It's done now." Geoff takes a sip of tea and pulls a face. "Not sweet enough."

"Sorry." I add a heaped teaspoon of sugar. "What about Ben? Does he know? And what will Muriel say?"

"What about them?" Geoff shrugs. "The money will pay for a few months' rent as well, while you go house-hunting. Ben's our only son, and it's *my* money, not Muriel's. I *want* to do it."

Geoff and I have never been close, but at this moment I need to hug him quite badly. I move forward awkwardly and put my arms around him.

"Thank you…I don't know what to say."

Geoff gives me a quick squeeze.

"Then say nothing. Least said, soonest mended."

***

Ben stirs when I return to the bedroom.

"Hi." I smile at him. "Your dad's transferred twenty thousand pounds to our bank account."

Ben yawns and sits up sluggishly.

"What?"

"I've just been speaking to him downstairs. We're twenty thousand pounds richer. We can rent for a few months while we look for a house."

"We can't take it." Ben shakes his head. "I don't want it."

"I've already gone through that with him." I reply. "He says he wants to do it and it's *his* money. Muriel doesn't know."

Ben lies back down and closes his eyes.

"I'll have a word with him tomorrow. Go back to sleep."

"I haven't *been* asleep yet."

Something tells me it's going to be a very long night.

Chapter Thirteen

Although I know renting is just dead money, I'm reasonably happy for the moment. I stand back and admire my efforts to furnish the front room at 650 Broad Walk, seemingly the longest residential street in Kidbrooke. Two armchairs secured from the Gatehouse charity warehouse are in good condition, and we've brought our TV over from Muriel and Geoff's place. The house already has carpets and curtains, and Muriel has given us a small coffee table to use.

Ben will be home soon, after he has prepared the next day's lesson. I have something to tell him, but am hesitant because he is still rather moody and we haven't ceased skirting around each other yet. However, I've stopped apologising; one can only be sorry for a certain amount of time before contrition turns to submission.

I hear his key turn in the lock, and walk to the hallway to greet him.

"Hi!"

I try to sound as cheerful as it's possible to be since Paul Cash darkened our doorstep three months' ago.

"Alright?" Ben gives me a nod. "Since the clocks went back I'm going to school in the dark and walking home in the dark too. I think I've turned into a mole."

These are the most words he's spoken to me in a long while. I keep a fixed smile on my face.

"Christmas holidays soon. The days will get longer after that."

He throws his briefcase down.

"Did you transfer the money back to Dad's account again?"

I nod.

"Yes. I wanted to speak to you about that... er... he's put the money back in the Nationwide. That's four times it's gone on its travels."

"I'm going round to speak to him tonight after dinner." Ben shakes his head. "This is madness."

"I'll come with you." I volunteer at once. "After all, I got us into this mess in the first place."

He stays tactfully silent on that particular subject, and pulls his mobile phone out of his pocket.

"I'll give Dad a ring and find out if it's okay for us to come over. I think they're coming back from Oxford Street at the moment after doing some Christmas shopping. Mum sent me a text earlier."

After speaking with his father, Ben seems in a better mood at last. I serve up his favourite dinner of steak and kidney pie and vegetables, and he wolfs it down appreciatively.

***

I tentatively put my hand in his after we park the car and walk the short distance up Glenhouse Road to Muriel and Geoff's house, which strangely enough is in darkness. Ben doesn't snatch his hand away and I'm encouraged further. I look at his profile as he gazes intently up at the front bedroom windows.

"That's odd. They said in the text that they'd be home by now."

The front garden, since turned into a car park by Geoff, is empty of Geoff's Audi and Muriel's Ford Kuga. We stride across the flagstones and up to the front door, which to my horror gives way at a push.

"I don't like this." Ben snatches away his hand and feels along the hallway for the light switch. "Something's not right."

The light illuminates a scene that I never want to see again as long as I live. Geoff, naked as the day he was born, lies at the foot of the stairs at an unnatural angle with terrible head injuries, and even to my unskilled eyes is obviously dead. I put a hand to my mouth.

"Oh God!"

Ben takes a momentary inward breath of horror, then grabs my sleeve.

"Don't touch him. Don't touch anything." He is surprisingly calm. "Wait here with me. I'm going to phone the police."

I feel sick and look away at the bloodied mess that is Geoff's head. Ben's hand shakes as he holds his mobile phone and dials 999 to speak to the operator. When he ends the call I wipe tears from my eyes and grab hold of Ben for comfort. My voice comes out as a whisper.

"Where's your mum?"

"I don't know." Ben's voice is shaky as he puts his arm around me. "Go and wait outside for the police. I'll have a look round to see if I can find her."

It's a relief to step outside into the cool evening air, away from the scene of carnage. I flop weakly down onto the low garden wall and look around me, to see that all the neighbours' curtains are closed against the night. A young couple snuggle together as they walk past me hand in hand, laughing at some private joke. Cars drive slowly along the road, which is full of parked cars on both sides. Life carries on as normal, while just a few feet away death has changed our lives forever.

***

There's a police station in the High Street, and so it doesn't take long before I hear the sound of a siren. I stand up and wave a squad car onto the front forecourt. Two burly officers in uniform step out of the car, and the next door neighbours' curtains twitch. One of the men comes forward.

"Mrs Hughes? I'm DI Steve Laming." He indicates with a finger towards his colleague. "And this is PC Simon Fielding."

I nod and blow my nose.

"It's terrible in there. My father-in-law is dead. My husband is looking upstairs for his mother, who is probably dead or injured too. We've not long arrived. They said we could visit tonight."

I reluctantly follow them back into the house. Ben comes down the stairs as pale as it's possible to be. He treads carefully over his father. Tears streak his cheeks.

"Mum's dead. Lots of stuff is missing. Whoever's done this has cleaned them out."

His eyes meet mine, and in that split second I know just as well as he does who the culprit is. I cannot believe this

80

is happening to me. I sink down to the floor and put my head in my hands.

Chapter Fourteen

One of the officers helps me to a chair in the front room. In a daze, I hear the other one on his police radio. I notice with a sinking feeling that the TV has been ripped from the wall, and Geoff's expensive stereo is missing. The Christmas tree has been knocked over, and several of Muriel's carefully-wrapped presents underneath it have all disappeared.

Within a short time photos are taken of the crime scene, and a doctor arrives to certify Geoff and Muriel dead before a private ambulance removes their bodies to a mortuary ready for autopsy. As Muriel is carried out in a black body bag, her washing machine cycle finishes and plays its usual silly tune. PC Fielding goes off to investigate, and I follow him and Ben into the kitchen.

"Did *you* turn the washing machine on?" PC Fielding looks at me.

I shake my head.

"No. Muriel must have done that earlier. Some of the cycles can take two or more hours."

I fantasise in my mind what might have happened as I open the door of the washing machine and remove the items of clothing inside. Muriel and Geoff must have disturbed a robbery taking place as they returned from London. Their house would have been in darkness as night fell at only four o'clock, and any opportunist thief passing by must have decided to break in.

But deep down I knew there was no opportunist thief champing at the bit to steal whatever he could lay his hands on. This was a planned burglary by somebody who had been watching the house for a long time, somebody like Paul Cash.

PC Fielding takes the clothes from my hands.

"Were the deceased wearing these today?"

Ben checks his phone and nods.

"Mum sent me a text earlier on from Oxford Street with a selfie. These are the clothes in the photo."

"We'll need to take them to help with our enquiries. Their attacker probably put these in for washing, but they may still contain some evidence."

I hear DI Laming's footsteps coming down the stairs, and his large frame fills the kitchen doorway. He looks at Ben and me.

"Forensics will take this place apart tomorrow, but for now it's best you give me a set of keys and go home. We'll do some house to house enquiries too, to see if the neighbours saw anything. You'll need to visit their bank and put a stop on all their cards. When you're given the death certificates you'll be able to close any accounts they have if you give them proof of who you are."

Ben nods.

"I have a joint account with my parents, so that'll be okay." He gives me a nudge, "You'd best tell what you know."

With a double helping of shame I relate the sorry tale of my ten thousand pound faux pas. DI Laming takes some notes and then we make our way to the front door. We're stunned; hardly able to believe Geoff and Muriel are dead and the house ransacked. When we walk outside, a little group of people have gathered on the pavement. Ben waves them away with one arm.

"Piss off and mind your own business!"

He holds out until we get home, then collapses in tears in one of the armchairs. I sit on his lap and put my arms around him. I'd do anything to turn the clock back.

***

A white-suited forensic team duck under a yellow cordon and drive off as we return the following evening. DI Laming seems out of place as he stands at the front door where Muriel and Geoff should have been. I hear Ben's intake of breath as he steels himself for what lies ahead. Geoff's blood still stains the hall carpet, and I look away.

"Good evening." DI Laming ushers us inside. "I had to call you back here so that you could have a walk around and make a list of what you think is missing."

"Yes, we can do that." I nod. "We lived here with Ben's parents for several years. Ben grew up here."

"Take your time." Laming thrusts two notebooks and pens in our hands. "I'd like a comprehensive list if possible."

Ben steps over his father's blood and onto the bottom step.

"I'll do upstairs."

With Laming shadowing me, I traipse around the rooms with my notebook to discover that only valuable items have been stolen which can easily be sold.

"They must have had a large van outside for some time." I remark, noticing a gap on the dining room carpet where an oak table used to stand. "Have you spoken to the neighbours?"

"Yes." Laming replies. "The woman opposite saw what looked like a rented van parked in the front garden when she drew her curtains, but she didn't think anything of it. We'll follow this up with car rental companies such as Enterprise and Europcar and the like. If you give me whichever phone numbers you have for your guy, then we can check whether any of them have been used to hire the van. Of course this may be just a random burglary. We've had a few in this area recently."

I nod despondently, while mentally stabbing Paul Cash several times, and then shooting him in the head. I feel so guilty as though I've personally killed Muriel and Geoff myself. I just want Ben to shout and scream and blame me for it all and get it over with, but he keeps his emotions in strict control as he makes several journeys around the rooms of his happy childhood, and with each trip the list of stolen goods increases.

Chapter Fifteen

I receive an email from Action For Fraud and my spirits rise until I read the message:

I am sorry that you have been a victim of crime. Thank you for taking the time to report it to Action For Fraud.

Experts at the National Fraud Intelligence Bureau (NFIB) review the information you provide and where possible match it against other available data, to enrich and corroborate the details of the fraud. The NFIB assess whether there are viable lines of enquiry that would enable a law enforcement organization, such as the police service, to investigate.

On this occasion the NFIB have reviewed your crime and, based on the information currently available, have not been able to identify a line of enquiry which a law enforcement organization in the UK could pursue.

We continuously assess the content of individual and linked crime reports. If, as a result of new information the situation changes, we will provide an update.

I am disappointed that nobody else has reported FinMoyle. I have to rest my hopes on the forensic team, who are extremely thorough and manage to obtain a couple of tenacious strands of hair off the clothes in the washing machine that do not belong to either Muriel or Geoff. There are no fingerprints to speak of around the house, but details of the stolen cars are released and we hold our breath.

I choose my moment to bring up a delicate subject as Ben and I sit down wearily to dinner a few weeks after the murders.

"What do you want to do with the house?"

Ben shrugs while chewing thoughtfully.

"Sell it, I suppose. The police are finished with it now. No way would I want to live there after what's happened anyway. I'm the main beneficiary in their will. I know, because they once told me."

His eyes are watery, and I'm reluctant to push the matter further. I feel wretched and suddenly cannot face any more food. Ben carries on speaking while I jettison my knife and fork and look down at the table.

"When the coroner releases their bodies for burial, I'm going to give them a good send off and then move away."

The singular 'I' causes my head to jolt up in surprise.

"On your own?" I try to chuckle but it doesn't work. "Don't you mean *we*?"

His reply shocks me to the core.

"No." He shakes his head. "I need some time alone to get my head around what you've done. I'm so fucking *angry* right now. I can't think straight."

That's it. With those few words he might as well just have told me that our short marriage is over. All my hopes and dreams of a roses-round-the-door country cottage with two flaxen haired children playing in the garden vanish in a puff of smoke from the cottage's non-existent chimney. His cold, impassive stare, so unlike the Ben I've known for the past seven years, freaks me out. In the depths of my misery I wrack my brain.

"I don't know what I can do to make it better. For all we know, your parents' deaths might not have anything to do with Paul Cash."

"Oh, grow up!" Ben gets to his feet in an instant and with one fell swoop pushes over the table, sending plates, crockery and glasses flying. "He'd probably been sitting outside their place with a bunch of mates casing the joint for weeks! I never knew you could be so stupid!"

Pasta sauce soaks into the beige carpet leaving a red stain, and I now wish I'd managed to eat all my spaghetti Bolognese. The discolouration grows wider with the addition of two half-filled glasses of Merlot. My lap is full of spaghetti and I find it hard to hold back a river of tears, but hold them back I do with the aid of much self- control. Ben turns around, storms upstairs, and slams the bedroom door loud enough to wake the dead.

***

On my hands and knees, I let my tears add an extra rinse while I scrub the carpet. Ben appears at the kitchen doorway, and out of the corner of my eye I see a suitcase in his hand. I pound the carpet in a furious spurt of energy.

"I'm going to clean up Mum and Dad's place, sort all their stuff out and get the house ready for selling. I'll be staying there for a while. The Christmas holidays will give me a chance to put their furniture in storage and give the walls a coat of paint."

I don't trust myself to speak, and so I remain silent and continue attacking a stubborn spot of sauce. For good effect I purposely turn my backside towards him as well. Ben's voice dampens any hope of a last minute reconciliation.

"See ya, then."

It's only when the front door clicks shut that the dams behind my eyes burst.

Chapter Sixteen

The children keep me busy until the end of term, but the upcoming two-week Christmas break stretches endlessly before me. On the twenty second of December I swallow my pride and make a phone call to the one person I know who will never turn me away.

"Hello Mum."

My eyes fill up again as my mother's cheery voice wends its way down the telephone line.

"Lauren! Lovely to hear from you! Are you and Ben coming down to see us over Christmas?"

"Just me I'm afraid." I try to reply in the same upbeat manner. "Ben needs to sort his parents' house out over the school holidays."

"Ah, I see. What a terrible business that was."

She doesn't know the half of it, and I have no intention of letting her know what a fool I've been.

"Can I come down tomorrow and stay for a week or so? Ben just wants to be on his own for his first Christmas without his mum and dad."

There's a slight hesitation at the other end.

"Oh, okay. Everything alright between you two?"

"Sure." I hope I can lie convincingly. "It's just that he's got a lot to do in order to put their house on the market."

"We'll look forward to seeing you then. Linda seems to have picked herself up a boyfriend at her university's end of term disco. He's coming over for Christmas dinner."

I feel a stab of envy. My quiet little sister is now grown up enough to sample the delights of dating and falling in and out of love. I'll be sitting there in the front room like a gooseberry, while she and her new fella get loved up on the settee. My life is unravelling faster than you can say *'scam'*.

***

DI Laming phones my mobile as I pack a case for Yorkshire.

"Happy Christmas." I say in a desultory tone. "What's the latest?"

Laming clears his throat.

"I've spoken to your husband. I just thought I'd better update you too, as he tells me you're not living together at the moment."

There's a pause while he waits for me to confirm or deny. When I do neither, he carries on.

We've had no sightings of your in-laws' cars. For all we know they may already be out of the country, but we'll keep looking. The DNA strands from the hairs don't match anything on our database."

"What about the rented van?" I reply. "Anything there?"

"Yes." I can hear no hint of hope in his voice. "One of the numbers you gave me matched somebody who called Thrifty Van Rental a couple of days before the murders. Seems they were calling on behalf of a company, Breenside Assets. The number is ex-directory of course, but we were able to trace it back to an industrial unit in Poplar, East London. The unit's now empty."

"Paul Cash... did he rent the van?"

I listen intently for his reply.

"Not that we know. We're following up leads, but at the moment it seems they've covered their backs pretty well. We're going to find out who owns the industrial unit and take it from there, but all offices on the estate where the unit is have now shut down for Christmas and there's nobody around to ask. All I can say is have a nice break, and we'll be on it first thing in January."

"Happy Christmas," I say with no real meaning. "Thanks for your work so far."

***

I pop a 'thinking of you' card through Muriel and Geoff's door on the way to the M25. The lights are on and I'm tempted to knock. However, I don't want to push my luck and inflame the situation even further. I can hear a DJ talking on the radio as I lift the letterbox, and suddenly remember there is no TV in the house thanks to Paul Cash. Unless Ben buys another one or the insurance company decides to pay out, I imagine he will be spending rather a cheerless Christmas. I yearn for forgiveness, but I must bide my time. I close the letterbox quietly, but to my relief the front door opens as I stride quickly over the tarmac.

"Thanks for the card. I'm painting the hallway."

Ben stands before me in his father's old paint-splattered overalls. I want to run towards him and throw my arms around his neck, but instead stand there by the garden wall grinning inanely.

"I thought I'd stop by on the way up to Yorkshire. I'm going to spend Christmas with my parents."

As soon as I'd finished speaking, I could have bitten out my tongue at the insensitive remark.

"Good for you." He replies without smiling. "At least you've got parents to spend Christmas *with*."

I edge further out into the street.

"I'm so sorry. I … I can't seem to do anything right. Please forgive me." I stand there mortified, waiting in vain for a response from Ben before continuing. "I'll go then. I think I'd better leave you in peace."

My eyes sting with a fresh river of tears as I run blindly to the car.

Chapter Seventeen

Linda opens the door, suddenly a young woman instead of the awkward teenager I remember from previously. Behind her stands a tall, gangly guy with a shock of bright ginger hair clipped neatly at the back but left longer on the top to fall down over his forehead in a fringe.

"Lauren!"

My sister hugs me more warmly than she's ever done before, and then turns to the youth.

"This is Chris. We met at Uni."

"Hi Chris." I shake his hand. "Pleased to meet you. I'm Linda's sister, Lauren."

Chris grins at me.

"We meet at last," he replies in a deep baritone. "I've heard all about you."

I step over the threshold and fling my case down.

"All good I hope?" I stifle a sigh at the thought of much forced jollity to come. "Where are the parentals, Lin?"

"Oh, they've gone to Tesco's to get some last-minute bits. I'll put the kettle on."

Chris follows Linda like a duckling, and I walk into the front room and flop down on the settee. Nothing ever changes much in Mum and Dad's house, and I'm suddenly glad of the familiarity. I gaze up at photos of myself and Linda on the wall over the fireplace, where Gran and Grandad also look down benignly. I wonder to myself whether they've ever met up on the 'other side', as they could never get along much on the earthly plane.

Linda returns and sets a steaming cup down in front of me on the table. Chris stretches his elongated frame out in one of Dad's armchairs and pulls the ring on a can of beer.

"Merry Christmas." Chris takes a swig and gives me a wink. "Don't worry, I haven't taken your bed."

I like the guy. He has huge feet, but I can see why Linda's fallen for him. He's affable and would get on like a house on fire with Ben, if only Ben were here.

"Glad to hear it." I reply with a mock-snooty air. "And I don't want to hear any creaking on the upstairs landing floorboards either."

"Lauren!" Linda throws a cushion at me. "Behave yourself!"

The phone buzzes in my pocket, and I take a welcome sip of coffee as Mum and Dad arrive at the front door.

"She's here!" Linda jumps up and runs out to the hallway. "Lauren's here, Mum!"

Everything must be alright, because my parents are home, and I'm home in my childhood house where nothing nasty ever happens to me. I give Mum and Dad a cuddle.

"Happy Christmas." I smell Mum's familiar scent and I want to bawl my eyes out. "It's good to be here."

Dad pats me on the shoulder, which is about as much as I can expect, and I kiss his cheek.

"I'm here for a week, if you can stand it."

"Don't talk daft." Dad ruffles my hair. "Make yourself at home."

When the family are in the kitchen unpacking shopping bags, I have the chance to check whether Ben has left a message. There's one voicemail from a withheld number, and as soon as I hear the familiar tones I feel a cold shiver run up my spine.

"Hello Lauren, it's Paul Cash. You've been a very naughty girl and changed your bank card, haven't you? Tut tut. Have a nice Christmas. I'll be in touch."

I can hear carol singers on the kitchen radio. I can't think straight. Ben is alone in the house where two horrific murders took place. Laughter floats along the hallway, and my in-laws' killer has just left a message on my phone. It's

98

Christmastime, the season of goodwill. Situation normal, all fouled up.

***

I grab my case and with the pretence of unpacking, run upstairs and dial Ben's number.

"What?"

He sounds tetchy and thoroughly pissed off.

"Ben, you have to listen to me."

"Go ahead." The voice is a monotone. "I'm listening."

"I've had a threatening voicemail from Paul Cash. He's found out I've changed my bank card. I opened up a new account and transferred the rest of the money. He says he'll be in touch."

"Tell the police." Ben replies. "They'll be able to trace the number."

My voice rises as I answer him.

"It's Christmas, and I'm in Yorkshire! Ben, you need to get out of that house. They might come back if they think I still live there! Go back to Broad Walk - I'm not there to bother you, and they don't know anything about it"

Ben is undeterred.

"There'll be somebody on the front desk. Phone and speak to them. You're fucking priceless, d'you know that?"

He's still angry as hell, but I need to know he's safe.

"Ben, I'm begging you!   Yes I'll phone the police station, but please don't stay there over Christmas."

He ends the call, and I dial DI Laming's direct number straight away but get through to the main desk.

"Hello. Can I help you?"

A   pleasant   female   voice   causes   me   much disappointment. I try not to sound like a mad woman.

"Please can I speak to DI Laming?"

Straight away I know what the answer will be, but try and hold out that hope might triumph.

"I'm sorry, he is not on duty until December the twenty seventh."

"PC Fielding?" I reply.

"I'll just put you through."

I am relieved that at least somebody knows what has happened. I explain my fears to the constable, who admits there are somewhat reduced staff levels over the Christmas period, but reiterates at least three times that any patrol car in the area will include Glenhouse Road on their route.

I'm about as far from reassured as it's possible to get.

Chapter Eighteen

If Mum and Dad notice anything amiss in my demeanour, they tactfully keep quiet and strive to keep the overall festive atmosphere painfully jolly. It helps of course to have my loved-up sister and her boyfriend about the house, as their romance is something we can all focus on rather than the murders of Muriel and Geoff.

I wake early on Christmas morning, and bleary-eyed check my phone for any text from Ben. However, the display screen shows no incoming calls or messages. I risk his wrath and compose a pitiful 'best wishes' diatribe, ending it with a row of kisses and a heart. There is no reply.

Mum serves up her usual sickening mince pies and cream for elevenses, and I want to gag as I force one down. Chris wolfs down four, and sends his compliments to the chef. Mum blushes like a schoolgirl.

Linda and I help out with the dinner preparations, while Dad and Chris shuffle off to the pub. I would have rather gone with them, but I know Mum would never let me hear the last of it. I chop carrots and parsnips and peel spuds while all the time thinking about what Ben might be doing back in Eltham. Linda throws a sprout at me when I absent-mindedly stir a cup of tea with a carrot baton.

"Hey! Earth to Lauren! Is anybody in?"

I look up from my reverie. Linda's face is radiant with the joys of Chris and Christmas, but all I want to do is crawl into a dark hole and hide from the world.

"Sorry." I smile at her. "I was miles away."

"Is everything okay between you and Ben?"

Linda is fishing for information, but I'm not one to air my dirty linen in public.

"Fine." I nod. "He just needs time over Christmas to sort his parents' house out."

"Did the police discover who did it?" Linda stops peeling sprouts and looks at me with interest. "Any clues?"

I shake my head.

"Not yet. Probably someone who had been watching their movements I expect."

I attack a pile of potatoes with gusto, and hope Linda is satisfied with my answer.

***

It's the first year since we've been together that I've had no Christmas present from Ben, but to be fair I didn't buy him one either. At least I sent him a card, even though I received nothing back in the post.

After playing happy families around the dinner table it's time to open presents. I try to show some enthusiasm when I'm faced with his and her cups from Linda, but it occurs to me that I may be the only one drinking from them in the future. Mum and Dad have bought us a voucher to exchange for a West End show and dinner for two. I hold the voucher in my hand and burst into tears. Mum runs over to where I'm folded in two on the floor and rocking back and forth in abject misery.

"Whatever's the matter, Lauren?"

I'm too upset to reply straight away, but instead let Mum hold me like she used to when I was a child. Dad and Chris look as though they'd like to be somewhere else. Linda skids across the floor and strokes my hair.

"S- sorry to dampen your day," I sob. "Ben and I aren't together at the moment. I did something really stupid, and in a roundabout way I think it probably caused the death of his parents."

There. I've said it. My dirty little secret is out. There's silence in the room as my outburst is inwardly digested. Mum is the first one to speak.

"Don't be silly. Whatever you've done, you've not murdered Muriel and Geoff."

"No." Linda chips in. "Somebody evil did that."

They're all too polite to ask what the hell it was that I did, and a blanket of gloom settles over the rest of Christmas Day. I try in vain not to spoil things any further, and make a superhuman effort to compose myself. When the aunts, uncles and cousins visit on Boxing Day and Linda goes off with Chris to visit his parents, I help Mum in the kitchen with the buffet lunch, while Dad plays the genial host and pours the relatives liberal amounts of sherry. Mum gives me one of her sideways glances as I arrange triangular ham sandwiches on a serving platter.

"Are you going to tell me the real reason why you're so unhappy?"

I break open packets of crisps and throw them in a bowl.

"I'm so ashamed." I sigh. "And so stupid."

Mum shakes her head.

"No, you're not stupid. No daughter of mine is stupid."

Dear Mum. She has no idea. I bring some jellies from the fridge and pour some cream into a jug. My mother still looks at me questioningly but keeps half an eye on preparing prawn vol-au-vents.

"You'll feel better if you get it off your chest."

The whole sorry scenario spurts out in an instant. Mum is right; I do feel a sense of relief afterwards that I'm not alone, and even manage a thin smile at Aunt Betty as I shove a plate of Twiglets under her nose. However, I'm not a child anymore, and this is one problem that Mum cannot make right again.

Chapter Nineteen

I drive back to Eltham with a heavy heart on the morning of the third of January, intending to make a quick scope of Glenhouse Road through the car's window. When I arrive there's an obvious police presence outside on the flagstones at Muriel and Geoff's house, and my heart begins to turn somersaults. I park in the road and let my feet move unwillingly towards number 79.

Has Ben suffered the same fate as his parents?

I ignore the twitching curtains opposite and let myself in with the key I've managed to hold on to. There's a smell of fresh paint, and the hall carpet has gone. I tread noisily over the floorboards to where DI Laming sits with a cup of tea in the front room opposite Ben, who doesn't even look up as I walk in.

"Hello." I look from one to the other. "What's happening?"

DI Laming gets to his feet.

"Good morning, Mrs Hughes. I just popped by with an update. We went over to Poplar yesterday and managed to track down the owner of several of the industrial units. He told me your man rented one unit for a couple of months but then left giving no forwarding address."

I look at Ben before replying. He stares at the carpet.

"What was he using it for? What name did he give?"

If Laming has noticed anything amiss between Ben and me, he remains tactfully neutral.

"The chap said it was rented in the name of Philip Carter, and they were using it to store and sell electrical goods."

"Yeah, all the stuff they'd nicked, I bet."

My head jolts up in surprise at the sound of Ben's voice. I try to make eye contact, but without success. Instead I ask a question that's popped into my head.

"Did the chap know they were going to leave so soon?"

"No." Laming shakes his head. "They'd paid rent for six months. We checked out the previous address Philip Carter had given, but the family living there had never heard of him. We'll keep following up leads though." He looks directly at me. "My colleague told me you've had a threatening message?"

I nod and let him listen to the message on my phone.

"Be aware of what's going on around you." Laming hands the phone back to me. "And be careful if you go out alone at night. It's probably best not to though. You have my direct dial number if you need me."

Laming finishes his tea and Ben sees him to the door. I'm not sure what to say to my husband, and so when he comes back into the room I wait for him to speak first.

"Had a nice Christmas then?"

His sarcasm is not lost on me. I shake my head.

"Horrible, actually. The worst ever."

"Really?" Ben flops down onto the settee so that his back is towards me. "I can't think why."

Suddenly I'm angry; angrier than I've been in a long time. His cold indifference combined with a week of worrying about whether Paul Cash had decided to make another visit to Glenhouse Road over Christmas tips me over the edge.

"*Fuck* you!" I shout. "I'm hurting too, and for your information I'm not a murderer! Yes I made a mistake and was taken in by that son of a bitch, but hey, nobody's perfect!"

He doesn't move from the settee. I turn and head for the door and slam it behind me with such force that one of the decorative panes shatters. Shards of glass fall around my feet. Full of remorse at my action, I look through a now empty square above the doorbell to see Ben's furious

108

eyes shooting hot daggers of hatred in my direction. With more self-control than I've ever possessed I back off and head towards my car, waiting for Ben to come running up behind me.

He doesn't.

***

Broad Walk looks the same as always. There are still Christmas lights in some of the gardens, but number 650 is in darkness. I walk up the path and turn my key in the lock. Cold air greets me as I pick up the post and switch on the hall light. I sigh. A new school term will soon begin, but it appears that the rest of 2019 won't be going quite to plan.

Chapter Twenty

The children are bursting to tell me all about the presents they received at Christmas. Their joie de vivre is infectious, and I can put my misery on the back burner for just a few hours. There's nothing quite like having to organize thirty five-year-olds for six hours to take your mind off your problems. Each child is totally self-centred, and their parents are not much better, some of them jostling each other after school ends to grab my attention before I leave the classroom.

There's one father I haven't seen before who takes his turn in the queue at three o'clock. He's olive skinned, swarthy and with a beard, and he's dressed in an expensive looking suit. I'm not sure which child belongs to him, as all the children have gone to run around the playground like wild things, happy to be let off the leash. He's last in the line, and just a few mothers are left outside chatting in the corridor. Suddenly it looks as though he's changed his mind about speaking to me as he follows the last mother out, but then my hackles rise as he closes the door behind her and turns to face me.

"Mrs Hughes?"

I'm nervous, but his voice is pleasant enough and it sounds vaguely familiar. He smiles and I relax a little as I sit in my chair and keep my desk between myself and him.

"Yes, that's me."

"I'm surprised you don't recognise my voice." He chuckles. "We've spent much time on the phone."

I've never phoned any of the parents in my short time at the school. I'm uneasy and let my chair slide on its wheels towards the panic button on the side of the blackboard.

"I've come to tell you that you've made a hundred and ten thousand pounds in profit from the London Liverpool merger. I tried to pay it directly into your bank, but you changed your bank details. I tried to phone you, but you didn't answer. All our calls are recorded for training purposes and if you remember, you mentioned that you worked in Wyefield School, and so… here I am with your profits. I took my six percent cut of course."

Paul Cash holds out a piece of paper that looks cheque-sized at the same time that Deborah Anderson knocks briefly and then opens the door.

"The cleaners will want to come in soon, Lauren."

I don't know what to do. My mind is spinning as I try and work out whether he is a genuine first class son of a

111

bitch or the genuine article. I blurt out the first reply I can think of.

"I just have to mark *Angela Draper's homework*."

Deborah's eyes dart from me to Paul, and then back to me again.

"Okay."

She retreats, and almost immediately I hear the faint click of the windows as they change into lock down mode. Paul, unaware, holds out his hand again and waves the cheque about.

"Come and get it! You thought I was a robbing bastard didn't you? Come on… admit it!"

He's laughing and I feel a complete fool. I've never held a cheque worth one hundred and ten thousand pounds before. I stand up and with my eyes fixed on the cheque, hold out my hand and walk over to the sand play area where Paul stands in his designer suit with a big grin on his face.

However, his firm grip is on my outstretched arm in an instant and I cannot break free. There an aroma of delicate but expensive lotion or aftershave. The cheque, if it was a cheque at all, is put back into his pocket and to my horror he now pulls out a knife from the inside of his jacket.

"Sorry darling, but I had to have a little laugh at your expense. You really must get out of the habit of being so trusting."

An icy terror lurches through my body as he holds the knife to the side of my neck.

"We're going to take a little drive to your bank. Two of my associates are waiting for your husband to return home, and so don't even think about alerting your colleagues. As soon as you draw out some more of your lovely savings, then I'll give them a call and we'll be on our merry way."

I nod and feel the blade scrape my skin.

"Please don't hurt us," I yelp. "I'll give you what you want."

Paul returns the knife to his jacket pocket.

"Then let's get on with it. " He opens the door and ushers me through. "After you, darling."

A couple of mothers are trying to open the main door at the end of the corridor without success as we walk towards them. Their children can be heard kicking the other side of the door from the playground. The mothers turn around to Deborah, who rushes from the office and talks to them in a low enough voice so as not to be heard by myself or Paul. Whatever she says instantly causes the women to panic. Their terror is visible on their faces as they run into the office behind Deborah. I know there's a good lock on the office door, and feel some relief that they've had time to shut themselves in.

"What's going on?" Paul has a vice-like grip on my arm as he runs more quickly along the corridor. "Who's locked the door?"

"It's in lockdown now!" I pant as I try and keep up with him. "You won't be able to get out!"

"We'll see about that!"

When we reach the office I can see three pale faces behind the narrow column of safety glass in the door. Paul swings an arm around my neck, and brings the knife out for the women to see.

"Open the fucking door or she'll get *this*!" He waggles the knife at them and then holds it to my neck. "Hurry up!"

"Lockdown can only be deactivated from the outside!" Deborah shouts out a reply and lifts her shoulders up in a despairing shrug. "It's been set up that way!"

For the briefest moment I have no idea why she is lying, and say a silent prayer as the blade presses against my carotid artery. The hurried lunch of prawn sandwiches and sponge cake churn around in my stomach, and my bowels and bladder scream for release. I know there is no way he could break any of the reinforced windows to get out.

"It's true!" I add for good measure. "Only somebody on the outside can do it!"

The grip around my neck intensifies and a trickle of urine runs down my leg.

"The children are outside!" I yell. "Get *them* to turn it off!"

"*You* get them to turn it off!" Paul shouts. "Do it *now*!"

"I need to go to the toilet first." I sob. "Look!"

I point downwards to a telltale puddle.

"My voice won't carry through the main door as well as yours. Let me go to the toilet and I'll tell you what to say."

"Don't think you'll escape, because I'll be standing there watching you."

If he gets his jollies watching me relieve myself, then I'm past caring. I sit on the toilet and hope I can think up an answer in time. I wipe myself, flush the toilet, and do what I must do to save my skin.

"They have to push the green button on the lintel above the office window, but they'll have to find something to stand on to reach it. Of course it was put up high in the first place so that the kids don't keep pressing it at playtime."

115

He pushes me to the main door while I struggle to zip up my trousers. He's fallen for it, and I hope against hope the police will arrive in time.

Chapter Twenty One

Paul barks out orders, but becomes increasingly frustrated at the inability of the two six year olds left out in the playground to reach the lintel. He drags me into a classroom, picks up a chair and hurls it at the window, which refuses to break.

"Fuck!"

The sound of police sirens fills the air, but I know he won't go down without a fight. He barricades us in behind a mountain of desks, then grabs me by the throat again when Deborah turns off the lockdown allowing a swarm of uniformed officers to rush in and stand outside the classroom. I can see one of them step forward through the glass panel.

"Come out with your hands above your head!"

The muscles in Paul's arm are rock solid, and I try not to panic at the thought of not being able to breathe if he squeezes any tighter. He waves the blade about in front of me and shouts to the police.

"I walk away, and she gets to live!"

I swallow hard at the rising bile in my throat. A voice from the other side of the door yells a reply.

"Come on out then!"

He's breathing harder as he switches the knife to his left hand and pulls out a phone, speaking quickly in a patois I cannot quite understand. I think of Ben held captive in his parents' house.

"I want to speak to my husband."

Paul ends the call and ignores my request. Keeping his left arm around my neck, he hurls desks and tables away from the door with his right hand, and stands facing the police through the glass panel.

"All of you … back off!"

The police shuffle backwards towards the main entrance. I am pulled hard against his left side as Paul gingerly opens the classroom door to a watching crowd of at least twenty police officers.

Before he has a chance to move the knife to his right hand, I bring my left knee up as hard as ever I can to make contact with Paul's testicles. In that split second as he struggles with a searing pain, three police officers rush forward to disarm him and pin him down onto the corridor's cold floor. I am so thankful to be free from his grip that I sink down to the ground beside them. When I

118

speak, my mouth is so dry that my voice comes out as a whisper.

"He's got people holding my husband Ben against his will at number seventy nine Glenhouse Road, Eltham. You need to get over there. They could be the ones who murdered Ben's parents!"

My message is noted, but after speaking I find my legs do not seem to belong to me anymore and I shake like an alcoholic with delirium tremens. Deborah rushes out of the office towards me and gives me a hug, followed by the two mothers who scoop up their offspring and rush away. Paul is dragged roughly to his feet and marched out of the door in handcuffs.

Out in the playground I can hear another siren, and an ambulance pulls up outside the door. Two paramedics in green coveralls run inside carrying large rucksacks of equipment.

"Are you hurt?"

I shake my head.

"I've wet myself." I sob. "I can't stop shaking!"

I'm cold. One paramedic places a silver foil blanket around me, while the other one goes outside and returns with a wheelchair. I put up no resistance as they lift me gently into the chair and wheel me out to the waiting ambulance.

***

I'm not sure if I was slipped a Mickey Finn, as who the hell can sleep on a hospital ward? I feel warmer when I wake up under blankets, and there's a visitor crashed out in an armchair next to the bed. Ben, with one black eye and a gash across his cheek, is gone to the world.

"He didn't want to be kept in overnight."

I rub my eyes and focus on a nurse standing at the end of the bed, and then again on Ben.

"Is he okay?"

"A few cuts and bruises, but he'll live. He wanted to be here when you woke up."

At her words my husband wakes from his slumber and looks at me with his one good eye. The nurse tactfully draws the curtains around my bed and then disappears.

"Hi." I smile at Ben. "How are you?"

"Fucking awful." He yawns. "How about you?"

I look down at myself.

"I don't remember changing into this gown. I peed myself, but then you would with a knife at your throat, wouldn't you?"

"You should've seen the police storm Mum and Dad's house. The neighbours will be talking about it for years."

"I'm so sorry about all of this." I shake my head. "It's all down to my stupidity and greed."

"I agree, but I do know that I was bloody lonely over Christmas without you, sitting in that house on my own."

I take his hand and lie back on the pillows, not taking my eyes off him.

"I've missed you so much, Ben."

He leans over and kisses my forehead.

"I've missed you too. I've been a holier-than-thou pig. What about we try again? I dare say you've learned your lesson, so I'm happy to say no more about it."

I sigh and squeeze his hand tighter.

"Thank you. No more Bitcoins. We'll work to get what we want."

He smiles at me. I have been given a second chance, and I'm going to grab it with both hands.

Chapter Twenty Two - One Month Later

Ben wants to check supermarket receipts. Previously he's never bothered about how much I spend on groceries, but now he asks to see what I've bought. I fight an increasing urge to bin the bloody receipt as I walk out of the store.

I want to prove that I'm a responsible adult. After work I stop off at the Nationwide to pay some of my wages into our savings account. When it's my turn at the counter I'm surprised to discover that just five hundred pounds are left. I pay in another three hundred, and drive back to Broad Walk to find that Ben has beaten me home. I take time to hang up my coat whilst thinking up the right thing to say in order not to cause a row.

"Hi." I smile at him. "Have you heard from the estate agents? Any interest in your parents' house yet?"

He gives me a quick kiss.

"There's been a few enquiries, but no takers."

I give him our savings book.

"I paid in another three hundred today, but now there's only eight hundred in there."

He scans the book and shrugs.

"I took the bulk out ready to pay fees for surveys and searches. You know ...all the expenses that come with buying a house."

I'm not convinced.

"Where's the money now?"

"I put it in an ISA" he replies and hands me back the book. "You get more interest that way."

"But I can access it online?" I look at him but he doesn't meet my eyes.

"Er... no." He shakes his head. "I've opened up a new bank account in my name."

A boiling rage bubbles up, but I keep a lid on it.

"So I'm not to be trusted with money then?"

He turns away and starts walking.

"I just need to know the money is there when we get the bills in. I'll want a full survey done on any house we buy, and that doesn't come cheap. Then there'll be carpets and curtains to buy. We'll need a few thousand quid for sure."

I stomp behind him into the front room.

"I made one mistake! God, I hope you're not going to hold that against me for the rest of my life!"

Ben sinks into an armchair and leans back onto the headrest.

"Of course not. Don't be a drama queen, Lauren. I'm just trying to get the best return for our savings."

I want to throw something at him. Instead I take a deep breath.

"I've got some lesson planning to do for tomorrow. Can you cook dinner?"

"Sure." He nods. "What's to eat?"

"It's all on the supermarket receipt." I cannot resist the riposte. "You'll have to scrutinise it again to see what you fancy cooking. Also it's probably best that *you* do the shopping now, but I'd like to see the receipt afterwards."

My heart is pounding as I run upstairs and sit at the computer. I'm angry as hell, and find it difficult to concentrate on tomorrow's lesson. Pretty soon a pleasant aroma of chicken and spices wafts up to the bedroom.

"Come and get it!"

I've done almost no work at all, and I'm hungry. I make a point of not looking at Ben as I take my place at the table opposite him.

"Cheers. It smells nice."

"We can do the shopping together." Ben replies. "Saturday afternoons work better for me after football practice."

I stab at a piece of chicken.

"When shall we start house-hunting?"

"It'll be best to wait until we get a buyer for Mum and Dad's place. Not everybody has five hundred thousand to burn. It might take some time."

I imagine half a million pounds sitting in his ISA and change the subject.

"Deborah's suggested counselling after everything that's happened. Do you think it's a good idea?"

"What for?" Ben shoves a spoonful of rice into his mouth. "They never offer advice anyway. They'll just sit there and say nothing and let you talk." He pulls a pseudo-sympathetic face. "How does it make you feel that you saw your parents butchered to death in their own house? Count me out. What a load of bollocks."

"Not only that." I gently venture. "Also the lack of trust... I – I don't think you trust me with money now."

He doesn't respond and we finish the meal in silence, while I vow to myself to open up a savings account in my name only. Two can play at that game.

Chapter Twenty Three – One Year Later

Somehow I found the strength to testify at Paul's trial, and even though he has been locked up at Her Majesty's pleasure for some considerable time, I still feel vulnerable. It has become extremely hard for me to stay behind after lessons end to speak to parents, and I dread meeting any father of a recalcitrant child. Deborah is very supportive however, and is always last to leave the building. Chatting to parents is part and parcel of the job of course, but now I find that I do not want to do this anymore.

Teaching was always my goal in life, and I worked hard for my degree. Now a combination of my own greed and Paul Cash has taken away the pleasure of it. My life is spiraling out of control. My husband is very wary of trusting me with any money, and I've become as bad as Ben in that I've taken all the remaining savings out of the Nationwide account and opened up an ISA in my own name. So far Ben either hasn't noticed or is not saying anything.

Every evening I look through job vacancies online and in our local newspapers while Ben marks books. It's got to the point where I'll do anything, even stack shelves in a supermarket, in order to feel safe.

Deborah doesn't want me to go, and it'll be a wrench to leave some of the kids for sure. However, with a certain amount of relief I give in my notice towards the end of the summer term, and haunt the local Job Centre in the afternoons. I accept the first offer that comes along; working back in Eltham as a library assistant. I gel with the librarian, Polly, straight away. The pay is down quite a bit, but I'm happy to get away from where Paul or his associates can find me. I know Ben isn't too pleased with my decision to leave teaching, and one night over dinner he makes it quite clear.

"Lauren, you've thrown your career path away."

I swallow a mouthful of shepherd's pie and regard my husband with some disdain.

"It's my decision. Who knows when they'll let him out? He would have been able to find me again if I hadn't gone."

Ben shrugs.

"So ... why didn't you move to another school?"

"There's still the parents to contend with." I reply. "Some don't take kindly to me telling them their little

Johnny is a real pain in the arse. Sadly, I feel that teaching isn't really right for me anymore."

Ben shakes his head.

"You can't let a low life like Paul Cash stop you from living your life."

"He isn't," I reply quickly. "I'm just living it a bit differently to how I'd first envisaged."

"Filing books and issuing fines. You don't need a Cambridge degree for *that*."

"It's called *shelving*, not filing. I'm going to have work-based training and study for an NVQ, and hopefully because I've already *got* a Cambridge degree I'll get to be a librarian after five years or so. And it's *not* just shelving books. Librarians have to look after all the electronic resources, and buy books, audio books, CDs and DVDs and stay within budget. I'm actually enjoying the work."

"Okay, okay." Ben chuckles. "You've made your point."

I smile at him and nod.

"Women are equal to men except for one thing and one thing only...physical strength. We girls have to be careful, as we were in the back of the queue when the Almighty was handing it out."

Ben laughs, and I get the feeling we might be back on a more even keel.

***

We've taken to cuddling on the settee while we watch TV, just like we used to do. It's easy at first to ignore my mobile phone vibrating with a call while Ben's hand fondles my breast, but the second time it happens I reluctantly pull away from him and pick up the phone to discover that the caller has withheld their number. I show the display screen to Ben.

"I don't know who it is."

"It might be the police or somebody from the estate agent's," Ben replies with a shrug. "You'd better answer it."

I press the 'Accept' button.

"Hello?"

"Am I speaking to Lauren Hughes?"

The masculine voice is deep and rather polite. I relax.

"Yep, that's me."

"Well, I just wanted to pass on a message from our mutual friend."

My blood runs cold.

"Who are you?"

"Doesn't matter about that. What does matter is that Paul is pissed off because he's in jail, and *you* put him in there."

I quickly end the call and throw the phone over to the furthest corner of the room.

"What's up?" Ben looks at me in alarm.

I take a deep breath and try to compose myself.

"That was one of Paul Cash's associates. We've got to move away, the sooner the better. The nightmare isn't over – I'm so sorry."

"Has he threatened you?" Ben replies.

"Not exactly." I cannot stop the trembling in my voice. "He just said that Paul is pissed off because I put him in jail."

"We *don't* move away." Ben shakes his head. "We stay put and fight. If push comes to shove we've got the police on our side. Destroy the phone and get a new one with a different number, and we'll get a new email address. They don't know we're renting this place, and you've left Wyefield School. I'm not spending the rest of my life looking over my shoulder."

I know he's right, but a sinking feeling comes over me just the same.

Chapter Twenty Four

We have an offer on Muriel and Geoff's place. It's not as much as Ben had hoped, but now we're anxious to sell up. The couple have four older children, and the house will be a perfect size for a larger family. They want to move from Durham due to the husband's job. I hope against hope they haven't spoken to any of the neighbours or read past local newspapers and discovered what's gone on in the house they want to buy.

By October I've been at the library a couple of months and have started my workplace training and NVQ course. I quite enjoy being on the front desk and meeting the public. The same sad faces tend to come in day after day; lonely elderly people in the mornings looking for somebody to talk at, harassed mothers and children after school ends, and working men and women for the evening shift. The work is boring and unsatisfactory. Every day I expect one of Paul Cash's cronies to walk through the door, and it's got to the point where I'm frequently living on tenterhooks. However, I'm surrounded by people all the time, and I do feel relatively safe. I have a new phone, and have changed my email address

Polly Sutcliffe, the Librarian, is rather astute; she's noticed how jumpy I am whenever the main door opens, and she wants to find out why. At our morning coffee break she gives me her best sympathetic face.

"Is Bert giving you trouble? I can't help but notice that sometimes you look downright terrified when a new reader makes their way to the front desk."

"Bert?" I reply with a blank stare. "Who's Bert?"

Polly grins.

"Oh, we have a stalker, Albert Watson. Have you not met him yet? He tends to favour young, pretty females. He was banned last year for crouching beneath the biographies with a mirror, but sometimes he chances his luck and comes back."

"Thankfully no." I shake my head. "Although I'm rather glad now that I prefer to wear trousers."

It's time to spill the beans. By the time I've related the sorry tale of Paul Cash's scam and its aftermath, my coffee has gone cold and I once again feel thoroughly depressed at my own stupidity.

"Don't worry, it's easily done." Polly gives me a reassuring smile. "I've lost money before to scammers as well. It takes a while to get over the anger."

As I go back to the front desk I muse over Polly's words. Yes, I *am* angry; a deep down boiling-over anger how faceless people in cyberworld can prey on fools like myself with pound signs in their eyes. Okay, Paul is now paying for his misdeeds, but how many other Pauls are out there currently fleecing poor old unsuspecting Joe Public?

***

We have completion on Muriel and Geoff's place a few weeks later, and after inheritance tax we finally have the money we need to buy a place of our own. My plans to get rich quickly nearly cost me my marriage, and now any future children we have will never know the love of their paternal grandparents. The whole experience has made me extra careful with money, and now, unfortunately I am much less trusting than before and more cynical.

I'm desperate to move far away, back to the security of Mum and Dad living nearby, and Linda and Chris. I miss my sister. I search the northern property markets and when I find the most wonderful house in Pately Bridge I cannot help but show Ben.

"What do you think? Mum and Dad don't live too far from there. We'll have *family*, Ben. I want our children to have *family* around them."

"They will." Ben sighs. "They'll have *us*."

It'll take some time, but I'm going to work on him. I want that house. I know that when Paul Cash gets out of prison he will not be able to find us, as we'll be living far away in Yorkshire.

Yes, I'm trying hard to put my life back together. Who knows, when we're in Yorkshire I may even go back to teaching. I have a vision of myself in one of those little village schools in the Dales, far away from the hustle and bustle of London. Mum will be on hand to be a doting granny, and over time I will do my best to win back my husband's trust. You live and learn, and boy, have I learned!

The End

OTHER BOOKS BY STEVIE TURNER

A HOUSE WITHOUT WINDOWS
A LONG SLEEP
A RATHER UNUSUAL ROMANCE
ALYS IN HUNGERLAND
BARREN
CRUISING DANGER
EXAMINING KITCHEN CUPBOARDS
FINDING DAVID: A PARANORMAL SHORT STORY
FOR THE SAKE OF A CHILD
HIS LADYSHIP
LEG-LESS AND CHALAZA
LIFE: 18 SHORT STORIES
LILY: A SHORT STORY
MIND GAMES
NO SEX PLEASE, I'M MENOPAUSAL!
PARTNERS IN TIME
REPENT AT LEISURE
REVENGE
SCAM!
THE DAUGHTER-IN-LAW SYNDROME
THE DONOR
THE NOISE EFFECT
THE PILATES CLASS
FALLING